"Do you know Mrs. Russell well?" Wade asked.

Megan met his gaze head-on, his dark brown eyes drawing her in. She imagined telling him all her secrets. She shook her head. Though it would be a relief to tell someone, sharing with a cop, especially now, would come under the heading of stupid.

"She's one of my best friends," Megan said. She wished she knew what he was thinking. "I didn't know her grandson very well at all, though. He's been back in town only a couple of weeks."

"But that isn't what you want to tell me."

Megan bowed her head, searching for the right words, knowing there wasn't anything except the bald truth. Finally she shook her head.

"You're going to think I killed him."

"Did you?" Such a calm question, those dark eyes still drawing her in.

"No." She swallowed. "But I told him that his grandmother would be better off if he was dead."

Books by Sharon Mignerey

Love Inspired Suspense

Through the Fire
Small Town Secrets
Shadows of Truth
From the Ashes

SHARON MIGNEREY

After living most of her life in Colorado, Sharon recently moved to the Texas Gulf coast where she found that southern hospitality lived up to its reputation for being warm and welcoming. She's always known that she wanted to be a storyteller from the time she learned that spelling words could be turned into stories. Sharon's first book was published in 1997 after winning RWA's Golden Heart award in 1995. That same book went on to win the National Readers' Choice Award. In addition to writing novels, Sharon has had several articles published by *The Writer* magazine. She says the accolades are wonderful, but the only lasting satisfaction comes from serving the work. When she's not writing, you can find her happily involved with her critique group, learning how to garden in the Texas heat, or playing with her two dogs.

Sharon loves hearing from readers. She can be reached either through her Web site (www.sharonmignerey.com) or in care of Steeple Hill Books, 233 Broadway, Suite 1001, New York, NY 10279.

the
good
neighbor

Sharon Mignerey

Steeple
Hill®

Published by Steeple Hill Books™

STEEPLE HILL BOOKS

Steeple
Hill®

ISBN-13: 978-0-373-44313-0
ISBN-10:   0-373-44313-7

THE GOOD NEIGHBOR

Copyright © 2008 by Sharon Mignerey

Printed in U.S.A.

Seest thou how faith wrought with his works, and by works was faith made perfect?
—*James* 2:22

For Daniele Seidner; critique partner, proofreader and most of all, friend—I would have never made it through this book without you.

ONE

This was the sort of morning that scrubbed the shadows from Megan Burke's heart. The sun peeked over Grand Mesa's ramparts east of town, golden rays spearing between houses and trees, leaves fluttering in the crisp breeze.

Definitely a TGIF kind of day.

Two of the patients on her schedule for today lived out of town, so she was looking forward to a long, beautiful drive through the autumn day under a brilliant turquoise sky.

Automatically giving thanks for the day the Lord had made, Megan locked her front door behind her and skipped down the steps, heading for the driveway, which hugged the boundary line of her small yard.

She set her bag of patient charts in the back seat of her car then went to the gate next to her garage.

After she rolled her trash can out to the curb, she went back for the recyclables.

Her neighbor Helen Russell waved to her from her kitchen window where she kept an eye on the comings and goings of the neighborhood. Megan waved back, hoping Helen wasn't as stressed as she'd been yesterday. As usual, Helen's cat sat on the windowsill, its gaze fixed unblinkingly on something in one of the trees whose large branches draped over the garage and driveway. Probably the regularly visiting raccoons that Megan had heard pulling over the garbage cans earlier. If they had, there would be a mess to clean up.

Helen disappeared, then opened the back door a second later. "Good morning, sweetie," she said. Deep smile lines creased the corners of her eyes. "It's sure a gorgeous morning." The cat rubbed against her legs, purring loudly.

"It is," Megan replied, thinking Helen sounded better today. She was glad for that. Her neighbor was the closest thing to family that Megan had, something she hadn't anticipated finding when she had moved here three years ago.

Helen's only living relative, her grandson, Robby, had returned to Natchez from Denver three weeks ago after losing his job. He had moved into Helen's basement bedroom and was trading heavily on his old reputation. He hadn't lived in Natchez in ten years, but was still regarded as one of the town's own, a status Megan doubted she'd achieve even if she lived here twenty years. Megan's concern was that Robby worried Helen with his late-night comings and goings, his loud music and his apparent lack of job prospects.

"How are the heads for our apple dolls looking this morning?" Along with several other people, Megan and Helen had peeled and carved over a hundred apples last night in Helen's inviting kitchen. To raise funds for the seniors' center, the dolls were going to be sold at the Apple Festival coming up at the end of the month.

"You should come see," Helen said with a smile. "Personality is beginning to pop out all over the place."

"Tonight," Megan promised, with a glance at her watch.

"Glenna Adams told me you were coming to see her today. She lived across the street, you know, until her husband retired. Poor thing. He died less than a year later," Helen said. "Does she still live with her daughter out in Granger Gulch?"

"She does." Megan responded as though this was the first time they'd had this identical conversation. Helen's lapses of memory had seemed worse over the past month, which had coincided with Robby's unexpected arrival. "And I'll be late if I get sidetracked."

"You don't need to worry about taking my trash out," Helen said. "Robby told me he'd do it when he left a little while ago."

Though Megan knew the trash barrel wasn't out by the curb, she looked back toward it anyway. "It's not there. It will just take me a minute to grab yours."

"That boy." Helen shook her head as though he really was a boy instead of a grown man in his midthirties.

"His car is still here," Megan added, "so he's probably still around somewhere."

Personally, she hoped he'd find someplace else to stay soon, since she was nearly positive he had been stealing from Helen. She had vast collections that included expensive jewelry, Italian ceramic figurines, hundreds of colorful, hand-painted pitchers from all over the world and a plastic washtub filled with old coins, some predating the Civil War. Every time she had been in Helen's house since Robby's arrival, he was asking his grandmother about her things and how much they were worth. Megan suspected his interest wasn't just a simple matter of curiosity.

"He came through the kitchen like a whirlwind about a half hour ago," Helen said. "He told me he had errands to run and that he'd be gone all day because he was checking out some prospects." She shook her head, her short, white curls bouncing a little. "I wish I understood what that meant. If he was applying for a job somewhere, why couldn't he say so?"

Helen had talked about that, too—Robby's job hunting or lack of it—every day.

Megan wished she knew how to tell her neighbor that Robby was stealing from her. Not an easy thing to do, since she couldn't prove it. Besides that, Helen saw him as needing sympathy because of his recent bad luck after losing his job in Denver.

"Is there anything you need today?" Megan asked. "I've got to stop at the grocery store on the way home."

"You're such a dear to ask, but no." Smiling, Helen gave a little wave, scooped up her cat and went back inside.

Megan headed for Helen's trash cans, her thoughts on her busy day as she pulled open the gate.

And there was Robby, sprawled on the ground next to an overturned trash barrel, a bloody gash at his temple, his sightless eyes fixed on the brilliant autumn sky.

* * *

His old stomach ulcer burning, Detective Wade Prescott arrived a half hour later at the address on Red Robin Lane in response to a personal call from the chief. Natchez, Colorado, had its first murder in more than thirty years.

Wade had moved here from Chicago six months ago to be closer to the vast expanse of wide-open spaces that had captured his imagination when he'd come to the area on vacation last year. He also wanted to live in a community where the crime rate was so low that he was the only detective in the county. The position had been described to him as more of a community outreach than an investigative job, and that had sounded perfect for a burned-out cop who had prayed to never investigate another murder. The one that haunted him daily had occurred twenty-two months ago, and involved two little girls who had been executed by their father and whose mother was now serving a life sentence for taking his life. The case had shaken Wade to the core, making him question whether he was fit to be a cop. Worse, he wanted to rage at God for the injustice of it all.

The houses in this older neighborhood were modest, with neat yards and big shade trees. The place was the quintessential small town. When he'd first moved here, he kept expecting to see Andy and Opie emerge from one of Natchez's tidy houses with their fishing poles over their shoulders.

He knew he was at the right place because of the people standing in clusters on the neighboring lawns. A police cruiser, a fire truck and an ambulance were parked in the middle of the street, effectively blocking traffic and adding to the chaos.

The first thing he noticed was a body bag and an old woman who couldn't take her eyes away from it.

A body bag. Surely some fool hadn't moved the body.

His gaze went back to the old woman who was being comforted by a much younger woman whose shirt and slacks were stained with blood. Both looked familiar to him, something that still surprised him even after six months. Natchez was a community of three thousand in such a remote part of the state the nearest city of any size was a three-hour drive away. That was undoubtedly why everyone had begun to look familiar—because he was seeing them all the time at places like the grocery store, the local diner and the Independence Day picnic. Firemen from the volunteer station were standing around, and the officer talking to them was Aaron

Moran, a rookie who had been on the squad a whole four weeks.

Moran came toward Wade as he got out of the car.

"I'm sure glad to see you," he said as another police cruiser drove up and a hearse from the funeral home parked behind Wade's vehicle.

"Where was the body found?" Wade asked.

"Over there by the trash cans," Moran answered, waving in the direction of a partially open gate with a rose-covered arbor. "The neighbor found the body when she went to take out Mrs. Russell's trash."

"Take Mrs. Russell inside," he told Moran, saving the talk about securing the crime scene and getting witness statements for a moment when he wasn't irritated. "Get her statement, and stay with her until I come get you."

He called to Officer Jim Udell, who was getting out of his cruiser. "Cordon off the crime scene," Wade told him, "starting there." He pointed to the curb about sixty feet in front of the gate. Then he headed down the driveway toward the young woman who was following Moran and Mrs. Russell into the house.

"Miss," Wade called to her.

She stopped, her vivid blue eyes filled with the dazed expression of someone unexpectedly exposed to violence. He felt an unexpected tug of sympathy for her. "You're the one who called this in?" he asked.

"Yes." Her gaze left his and drifted to the body bag.

"I need to talk to you." Noticing a picnic table under an umbrella in the backyard, he waved toward it. "Do you mind waiting for me over there? I shouldn't be more than five minutes."

He'd had years of experience securing people's cooperation—just the right amount of authority in his voice without making people afraid. Yet, she reacted to him as though he had shouted at her. She was pretty, something he noticed as a man more than as a cop, a notion that didn't please him a bit, as he studied her face. There was a time and a place, and this was neither.

Her shocky expression faded a bit. With a nod, she walked away from him, leaving him with the feeling there was more to her than a neighbor simply finding a body. Tucking away that thought to reexamine later, he turned back toward the chaos, determined to get control of the crime scene.

Firemen, EMTs, a couple of guys from the funeral home, and the county coroner were the only other people left inside the perimeter that Officer Udell had blocked off with crime-scene tape. "Talk to the folks standing around," Wade told him, "and see what they saw or heard. Find out who belongs on this street and who doesn't."

"I'm on it," Udell said.

Doc Wagner, a family practitioner who had first been elected as the county coroner close to forty years ago, came toward him. Since there wasn't much crime in Natchez, there was no medical examiner to help investigate and make sure evidence was preserved—just this family doctor who was a fixture in the community.

"Just need your okay to hand the body over to the mortuary and I'll get out of your hair," Doc Wagner said, smiling as if it was already a done deal.

"Can you hang around for another minute?" Wade asked, doing his level best to hide his irritation. How could the man not know to leave the body alone?

Without waiting for an answer, he headed for the firemen. "Are you guys finished up here?" he said, instead of demanding that they get out of his crime scene.

"Who are you?" one of them asked.

"Detective Wade Prescott," he answered, flashing his badge. "Clearing the crime scene so I can start my work."

"I know this guy," the fireman said, pointing at the body bag. "We went to school together."

"Yeah?" Wade reached for the notebook in the pocket of his jacket. "What's your name?"

"Brian Davis." The firefighter stuck out his hand. "You're the new guy on the force."

"I am." That came up daily. "What can you tell me about Mr. Russell?"

"Robby?"

Wade looked at the name he'd written down when the chief had called him. "That's right."

"Haven't seen much of him lately, but he grew up right here in that house. His grandmother raised him."

"When was the last time you spoke to him?"

Davis stared at the ground a moment before answering. "Couldn't tell you for sure. Probably a couple of years. I'd heard he was back in town, but our paths hadn't crossed, you know?"

Which meant this witness couldn't help nail down the events leading up to the murder. Wade took down the phone number and other contact information, aware that Doc Wagner was calling to him.

Turning back to the coroner, Wade led him toward the body bag. "You couldn't wait until I got here before you moved the body?" Wade knew his tone was too sharp, but didn't care. Bodies didn't go anywhere, and you got only one chance at the physical evidence. This crime scene was so contaminated, he didn't know how he was going to figure out what had happened, much less make a case.

"I couldn't leave him out here in plain sight of his grandmother," the doctor responded, clearly irritated. "Dead or not—"

"This is your first murder?"

Doc Wagner was long past seventy and was exactly what you'd expect a family doctor of his generation to look like. "No," he said. "The last one was five years ago. Hasn't been one inside the Natchez city limits, though, in a long time."

"The crime scene is mine," Wade said. "Nothing gets moved until I clear it."

"And the body is mine," the doctor said. "I'd be happy to show you the state statute that says it is."

"Maybe. But where I come from, we don't move anything until we're sure the evidence is preserved."

Wagner's eyes glinted and he straightened to his full height. "I determined the cause of death."

Wade knew he wouldn't have that for sure until after the autopsy, but there was no point in arguing right now, especially when he looked toward the backyard and saw his witness watching them. "Which was?"

"Blunt-force trauma to the head." The doctor waved in the direction of the half-open gate and the overturned trash cans. "Looks like a garden spade back there was the murder weapon." He took a breath then continued, "I might not be some young, big-city detective who's up on all the latest. But I know you can't leave a dead man around for all the gawkers. And, I couldn't stand that Helen was so upset."

"Next time, move the gawkers, not the body," Wade said, figuring this would be only the beginning of the criticism. He was bound to step on a lot of toes before the day was over. "I don't suppose you thought to take any pictures."

Looking baffled, Doc Wagner shook his head, making Wade wonder if he had ever attended any continuing-education classes in forensic science since being elected. Murder 101. Do not move the body. Even one of the bad police dramas on television ought to have clued him in.

At the moment, Wade wished this really was one of those dramas. Give him an hour, and he would have corralled all the witnesses, uncovered all the evidence, foiled the killer before he made his escape or killed again, and kissed his pretty witness, all before heading home for a good night's sleep. Yeah. And pigs could fly.

From her seat at the patio table, Megan watched the detective take charge and thin out the throng of people that had shown up after she had called 9-1-1.

Megan's regret was that Helen had seen, and she kept wishing that she had thought to cover the body. Megan knew from personal experience how devastating losing a family member in a violent death was. There was no erasing that image, no matter how much time passed. She knew because she'd been carrying one for nearly twenty years. Sometimes it was so vivid that it might have been yesterday.

Don't go there, she warned herself, focusing on the detective as he talked to Doc Wagner. She vaguely remembered reading an article about him in the *Gazette* when he had been hired last spring. He wasn't as old as she had imagined someone with his experience would be, though he certainly had a hard-edged look. His piercing gaze roved constantly over the yard as though he was memorizing the scene in addition to listening to Doc. She couldn't hear what they were saying to each other, but from the set of the detective's jaw and shoulders, she suspected that he was irritated.

Megan knew from her own training that Robby's body shouldn't have been moved, though at the time, helping Doc had seemed the sensible thing to do. She wasn't sure how she was going to explain that to the detective. Actually, there were a lot of things she wasn't sure how to explain to the detective.

"God help me," she whispered under her breath as he came toward her, unsure whether it was prayer or lament. As for the prayers, she knew she'd have a lot of those later.

He smiled when he reached her. "I'm Detective Wade Prescott," he said. "You're Mrs. Russell's neighbor?"

"Yes. Megan Burke."

"Do you mind if I sit down?"

She shook her head, and he settled into the chair next to her, taking in Helen's colorful back-yard. Megan looked, too, wondering if he saw the yard the way she did—a well-cared-for sanctuary where murder should never be thought of, much less committed.

"Somebody is quite the gardener," he said. "I've never seen more beautiful roses."

"They are Helen's pride and joy," Megan said, wishing he'd skip the small talk and get to the point.

"You know her well?" he asked.

"She brought me a loaf of freshly baked bread the day I moved in three years ago and I've talked to her almost every single day since."

Megan met his gaze head-on. His dark brown eyes drew her in, the expression there so interested, so focused, she imagined telling him all her secrets. Though it would be a relief to tell someone, sharing with a cop, especially now, would fall under the heading of "stupid." He cocked his head to the side as though waiting to hear what she'd say next, his dark hair falling across his forehead.

"She's one of my favorite people," Megan said. She met his gaze, wished she knew what he was thinking. "Aren't you going to ask about Robby?"

"Okay," he agreed. "What about him?"

"I don't—didn't—know him very well at all. He's been back in town only a couple of weeks."

"But that isn't what you want to tell me."

It wasn't.

Megan bowed her head, searching for the right words, knowing there wasn't anything except the bald truth. Finally she shook her head.

"You're going to think I killed him."

"Did you?" Such a calm question, those dark eyes still drawing her in.

"No." She swallowed. "But I told him that his grandmother would be better off if he were dead."

TWO

Megan's statement echoed in Wade's head as he looked at her. She had a girl-next-door wholesomeness about her that he knew from experience was usually only skin-deep. For some reason, he wanted Megan to be what she seemed. Of course, he had hoped to spend the next fifteen years of his career without investigating another murder.

Clearly that wasn't going to happen.

Her dark blond hair was sun-streaked as though she spent a lot of time outside. At the moment, though, she was pale, the sprinkle of freckles across her nose and cheeks clearly visible. Her hands were clasped, probably to keep them from trembling. All the classic and expected things of a witness in this circumstance. But, her own words took her from witness to suspect.

She held his gaze steadily without saying anything further, which intrigued him. Most people couldn't stand the silence and were eager to fill it up. Not this woman, though. She didn't look away, but there was nothing defiant in her gaze. All Wade heard was the murmur of voices beyond them and the chirp of a bird in a nearby tree.

Finally, he cleared his throat. "I suppose you're going to tell me that it was one of those things you say in jest when you're mildly annoyed." He never spoke first. It was a cardinal rule of his, one he was acutely aware of breaking.

Then, she did look away, her gaze moving toward the backyard, a shimmer appearing in her eyes. "No," she whispered. "I've never— I don't say things like that."

She never what? He wondered even as he acknowledged that she was telling him she'd been serious about the threat. He'd given her a way out, and she hadn't taken it.

"Maybe you should just tell me how it happened. Give me some context to work with."

Those vivid eyes fastened on him once more, and he realized her lashes were the longest he had ever seen. She really did have beautiful eyes. If he were to trust the old saying that eyes are a window to the soul, then this woman was innocent. Tempting, but he knew better.

He looked away from her face, studying the blood on her clothes. Though it would take a forensic examination to know for sure, his study now matched his first impression—there was no blood spatter from a live wound, but instead smears that might have come from touching someone you hoped would still be alive.

"Where do you work?" he asked, looking at a vaguely familiar emblem embroidered on the pocket of her shirt—a pair of hands cupped beneath a loaf of bread.

"Our Daily Bread," she answered, giving him the name of a local home-health-care agency and making him wonder what she did there, since he'd already met several of the nurses and the PA. She touched her forehead with her palm. "I've got to call in. I was due at my first patient's house a long time ago."

"You're a nurse?"

"A physical therapist. I work with patients who can't get to the rehab center at the nursing home." She reached for the clip on her belt that held her cell phone.

"Why is that body still lying out here?" The sonorous voice of Wade's boss, Chief Carl Egan suddenly carried toward them.

Wade looked up to see the chief coming toward

him, his eyes shadowed by the brim of the black baseball cap he always wore.

"There you are, Prescott. What do we have so far?"

"Maybe now is a good time to make that call," Wade said to Megan. "I'll be back." Standing, he headed for the driveway, leading the chief away from his witness. "The body is still here because I haven't examined it yet," he said.

"And why not?"

"It's not going anywhere. Not like other evidence and witnesses."

"Uh-huh. Continue." Though Egan's tone was curt, he relaxed a little, folding his arms over his chest and rocking back on his heels the way he did when he was concentrating.

"At the moment, we're taking witness statements and doing the initial neighborhood canvas. As soon as we're done, we'll begin processing the crime scene."

The chief lifted his hat, scratching his nearly bald head. "You can't just leave a corpse lying out here in the driveway. This is a small town, Prescott. People aren't used—"

"The body was like that when I got here," Wade said. "So I don't have any context for the crime scene." He nodded toward Megan. "She's the one who found him, and in a minute, I'm going to get her to show me exactly where and how."

"Well, get to it, Prescott. You're my expert, but I can tell you, you've already ruffled a few feathers. Doc Wagner called me up while I was on my way over here and bent my ear about the way you've run roughshod over everyone."

Wade didn't bother correcting that, but said, "Maybe he should have thought of that before he moved the body."

The chief's head came up and he looked back toward Wagner. "He did that?"

"He did."

"Well. That does color things a little different now, doesn't it?"

"We've got a mess," Wade added. "Since the body was moved, I don't yet know whether the victim died here or somewhere else. I don't even know for sure that it was a murder, though at least one person evidently made a threat against him. But there were so many people moving through the area and contaminating the scene that this investigation is going to be a problem."

"Hang on a minute. You've already talked to a suspect?"

"Witness," Wade corrected.

"Well, bring him down to the station. Who is it?"

Egan asked, remaining fixed on the idea of a suspect and a quick resolution to the case. Wade understood the agenda since it was the same with police chiefs everywhere. The quicker a case was solved, the less fallout there would be.

"A witness," Wade repeated, nodding toward Megan. "Mrs. Russell's neighbor."

"The gal who found him?" The chief looked in her direction. "I'll take her down to the station and put her in holding. You want to be there for the interrogation?"

"I'd like to get her statement before we accuse her of anything that, at this point, is pure conjecture," Wade said. "And, since she's the one who called this in, I want her to tell me how she found the body. Then you can take her." He glanced back at Megan. "We'll need her clothes, too." Wade paused, waiting for Chief Egan to look back at him. "You know that witnesses to this kind of crime sometimes have post-traumatic stress symptoms that makes them look like they have things to hide when they don't."

"I've done my share of interrogations, Detective," the chief said stiffly.

"All I'm saying is maybe we want to take it easy with her. See where it leads us."

Chief Egan nodded. "Smart. Get her to convict herself with her own words." He glanced back toward Doc Wagner. "You talk to your suspect and I'll get Doc Wagner settled down. The sooner you can release the body to him, the better."

"The body needs to go to Grand Junction for an autopsy by the medical examiner, in case this goes to court. We'll need this done by a certified professional."

Egan stared into space a moment. "That's spreading resources pretty thin, since we'll need to send an officer along to keep the chain of evidence intact."

"That's right." Wade looked toward Doc Wagner, who was still talking on his cell phone. "Like the man told me, the body is his by state statute. As coroner, he can accompany it."

Chief Egan laughed. "Nothing like getting even for messing with your crime scene, is there? Okay." He slapped Wade on the back. "I'll talk to him."

By the time Wade headed back toward her, Megan had finished her call. Her boss, Sarah Moran, had told her not to worry about a thing, saying that she'd notify all the patients on Megan's schedule for the day.

Detective Prescott's posture was all tense again, she noted, deliberately thinking of him by his title. Finding that her hands were once more trembling, she clasped them on top of the table. She remembered this from before, and it seemed to her that she'd spent a long time shaking, especially when she had tried to go to sleep.

Stop it, she mentally scolded herself. She was no longer a child, and she'd be able to handle this.

"Are you up to showing me how you found the body?" he asked, pulling out a notebook from the inside pocket of his jacket and coming to a stop a few feet away from her.

She stood and came toward him, determined to get everything out in the open. Better he hear it from her than someone else. "I helped Doc Wagner put him—Robby—in the body bag."

He looked at her steadily as though she'd simply told him something banal, like it was a nice day. "Is that when you got the blood all over you?"

She looked down at herself. "I don't honestly remember." How could she have not noticed the blood before now? "I remember touching Robby's neck to see if there was a pulse. There wasn't."

Over the next few minutes she explained to Wade how she had found Robby while he drew a sketch, adjusting the lines on the drawing as she struggled to remember as many details of those awful minutes as she could.

When they were finished, he thanked her, then said, "We need to get a formal statement from you, and for that, Chief Egan is going to take you down to the station." He paused. "And, we're going to need your clothes as possible evidence, so he's going to go inside your house with you while you get something to change into after you get to the station."

Megan felt her lips go numb. This was more than a witness statement. "Am I a suspect?"

He seemed to weigh his words before answering without anything close to a reassuring smile to ease his somber expression. "Let's take this one step at a time, Megan." He said her name the way a friend might, only she knew he wasn't, couldn't be, her friend. "The sooner we get your statement and process the crime scene, the sooner we'll have an idea of who did this."

With that, he introduced her to Chief Egan, whom she had seen at quite a few different civic functions over the last three years. If he recognized her, he didn't indicate it at all. He was silent as they went inside her house and she retrieved clothes to change into.

As stern as Detective Wade Prescott had seemed to her, Chief Egan was even more so, his gaze avoiding hers as she climbed into the back seat of his cruiser. When he closed the door, she looked across the street to the shocked faces of her neighbors. Was it her own rampant imagination, or had their eyes narrowed in suspicion? She wanted to bow her head and cry, but instead she lifted her chin, managed what she hoped would pass for a re-assuring smile and waved at them. Only Angie Williams, her youngest child riding on her hip, waved back.

On the short drive to the police station, Chief Egan was quiet, his gaze meeting hers in the rearview mirror only once. When they arrived, he barked an order to Caroline York, the dispatcher, to accompany her to the restroom where she was to collect Megan's clothes.

"Hi, Caroline," Megan said as the woman came around her desk.

"I'm so sorry for what happened this morning," Caroline responded. "Are you okay?"

"Wait," Chief Egan said. "You two know each other?"

"Sure," Caroline said. "We go to the same church."

"Uh-huh," he said, narrowing his eyes. "You're the only female on duty today, so you're stuck with collecting the evidence whether she's a friend or not. Understood?"

"Yes," she replied evenly, leading Megan down the hall and rolling her eyes when they were out of sight of Chief Egan. "My gosh, he's acting as if you're a suspect, instead of the person who reported the crime."

Megan didn't say anything about the chief. Instead, she asked Caroline, "How's your grandfather?" He had been a patient last winter when he'd suffered a mild stroke.

"Testy as ever," Caroline replied in her cheerful tone. "He likes making me think that he doesn't want Billy and me living with him. And I'd almost believe him if he didn't light up like Christmas when Billy gets home from school. Billy can't wait to show his great-grandpa his papers, and Gramps can't wait to see them."

Caroline's description of a family that took care of one another, even as they meddled and interfered in one another's lives, made Megan envious. She thought of the void in her own life. Helen Russell was the closest thing she had to a mother, a bond that was sure to be tested when the old woman found out how much Megan had disliked and distrusted her grandson—a man who was no longer here to tell his side of the story.

"You're awfully quiet back there," Caroline added as Megan passed her bloodied shirt and pants over the bathroom stall. "Are you sure you're okay?"

"I'm fine," Megan said.

"Is there anyone I can call for you?" Caroline asked.

"I'm worried about my neighbor, Helen Russell.

If you could call Reverend Ford and ask him to check on her, that would be great."

"Consider it done." She paused, then asked, "What about you? Anyone I can call for you?"

"No, but thanks, Caroline." Megan emerged from the stall as Caroline carefully labeled the paper bags she had put Megan's clothes in. "What's going to happen with my clothes?"

"You'll have to ask Detective Prescott. He's sure a stickler for making sure everything is packaged just so. We all had to sit in on training just last week." She frowned. "With all this, I guess it's a good thing we have a system."

"Hey, enough of the chitchat!" Chief Egan called from outside the door.

Shaking her head in disapproval at his tone, Caroline pushed open the door. Chief Egan stood in the hallway, his arms folded over his chest. "Ms. Burke, you'll wait in here." He pointed toward a conference room.

Relief feathered through her chest—she had been sure that she was on her way to jail.

"Maybe she'd like a cup of coffee, Chief," Caroline said.

He scowled, then asked, "Would you?"

"Yes, please," Megan said as much to goad him as because she really did. "With cream."

"I've got some half-and-half in the back instead of that icky powdered stuff the officers use," Caroline said. "I'll get it after I lock this up." She held up the paper bags and disappeared down the hallway while Chief Egan waited pointedly next to the conference room door.

"So you and Caroline are friends," he said to Megan.

"We are." Not close ones, but no reason to admit that at the moment.

"Uh-huh," he said, motioning Megan into the room.

Megan went to the end of the table and chose a chair that let her look out into the front of the building. She hoped she looked calm, but the truth was, inside she felt as though she was shattering into a gazillion little pieces. The truth was that inside she felt like she was eleven again, a child whose whole world had shattered.

Looking out the window to the street beyond, she was able to reassure herself that she was not in Hackensack, New Jersey. She closed her eyes, deliberately recalling each of the businesses on the block across the street. This was Natchez, the town that had been her home for the past three years.

"Here's your coffee," came Caroline's bright voice. She breezed through the door past Chief

Egan, a coffee mug in one hand and a pint of half-and-half in the other.

"Thanks." Megan poured it into the mug filled with coffee, watching the two liquids merge together before handing the carton back to Caroline. Beyond her, Chief Egan gave the dispatcher a curt nod, urging her out of the room.

Then he crossed the room and sat down across from Megan.

"My new detective said he wanted to be here for your statement," he said. "Do you want to call a lawyer?"

She knew what he was really saying—that he thought she had killed Robby—and she also knew she probably *should* call a lawyer. Instead, she wrapped her trembling hands around the warm coffee, raised her chin, and met his gaze. "If you're accusing me of anything, you need to be a lot more direct."

"When the time comes to Mirandize you, you'll know it."

She met his gaze without answering.

"And you're not hiding anything," he added, his tone too flat for the sarcastic words.

She wasn't, at least not in the way he meant.

"You'd better pray you have your story straight by the time Detective Prescott gets here," Egan said, closing and locking the door behind him as he strode toward the front door.

This wasn't quite jail—not like it had been the last time she'd been accused of murder.

THREE

Three hours later and with his frustration level mounting, Wade came through the front door of the police station. Just as he had been afraid of, the crime scene had not yielded any obvious evidence that could set him on a logical path forward. Forensics might turn up something, but he couldn't count on it. The probable murder weapon, a garden spade, had smeared fingerprints on it, as did the lid of one of the garbage cans. The only other interesting things discovered were some old coins next to scuffed footprints that were near the back fence behind the garage. At the moment, he had no idea if those were connected to the crime.

All he wanted to do was go home where he could lose himself in the hard, physical labor of turning over the caked red dirt that passed for soil in his backyard. Caroline said hi from her place at the front desk as he paused to pick up messages from the credenza behind her.

"Chief wants to see you," she said. "And Megan Burke is still here."

"Thanks," he automatically said, pushing through the gate that separated the front of the office from the bull pen where his desk was. His gaze lit on the glass-encased conference room across from Chief Egan's office. Megan sat at the head of the table, her gaze focused on the door he'd just come through. She looked directly at him. As intensely as had happened when he'd met her this morning, he had that punch in the chest of pure, male interest. He'd been here six months, working only a couple of blocks from where she worked, and he'd never seen her until this morning. He wished that he'd met her some other way.

But wishes, like prayers, were futile things.

With that he reminded himself of the big reasons to shelve his interest until he forgot about her. She was his probable best witness in a major case, possibly a major suspect. If that wasn't enough, all he had to do was remind himself of the nightmares that haunted him, which didn't mix with a relationship. At the turn of his thoughts, he gave himself a mental shake. He'd gone from thinking the woman was pretty to planning a life with her in a single bound. Irrational *and* stupid.

Across the hall from the conference room door, Chief Egan sat behind his desk, his feet propped on the credenza behind him, and a telephone receiver tucked between his ear and his shoulder. Their eyes caught in the reflection of the glass doors above the credenza. He waved at Wade to come into his office, dropping his feet to the floor and turning to face his desk.

Glancing a last time at Megan, Wade headed for Egan's office. He ended the call with whomever he was talking to and resettled the baseball cap on his head. He pushed several sheets of paper across the desk toward Wade.

"I've had a couple of interesting phone calls," Egan said as Wade picked up the sheets. "Your suspect—"

"Witness," Wade corrected.

"—had a very public and heated argument with the victim a couple of days ago in front of the pawnshop." Egan waved toward the sheets. "I took Thomas Johansen's initial statement."

"Of Johansen's Pharmacy?"

"That's right. I've known the man for thirty years, and he's as trustworthy an individual as you could ever find."

A good trait to have, Wade thought, since he wouldn't want an untrustworthy pharmacist to fill his prescriptions.

"Anyway, the vic accused Ms. Burke of being a gold digger and she told him that he was no good and that Helen Russell didn't deserve the kind of heartache he was putting her through. According to Johansen, she also told him that she wished he'd never come here and that Mrs. Russell was better off without him." He waved toward the sheets of paper once again. "Mrs. Russell's most recent bank statements are in there. Never knew before the lady was richer than Midas, so we've got our motive."

Wade had spent more than an hour with the lady, and he'd come away with the impression that she lived comfortably. If she was wealthy, she wouldn't be the first person he'd met who lived far more simply than their bank account permitted. He did understand where Egan's thinking had headed; however, as he turned to look out the door and across the hall where he could see Megan. "You think she's after Mrs. Russell's money and killed the grandson to get it?"

Egan nodded. "We've got to start somewhere, and that motive makes sense. That young lady drives a Lexus RX, has a pot full of money in savings, and a job that wouldn't appear to support having either one. I figure the vic was onto something. She makes friends with these old people, gets in their good graces, and steals from them while everyone is smiling. She killed the grandson to squash his accusation."

"Got any evidence to support that theory?" Wade asked.

"That's why I've got you, Detective. To find it."

Wade stared at his boss a long moment, remembering all the other times he'd been pressured to button up a case and get the public settled down. Too well, he knew the cost of putting the wrong person in jail.

Wade stepped into the office and closed the door. "Since this is the first major case we're on together," he said, setting the papers on the corner of the desk, "a reminder about how I work. I follow the evidence where it leads me, not where anyone with an agenda wants it to go. If it proves a theory, fine. If it doesn't, fine."

"I get your drift." Egan pointed at the glass door of his office, through which there was a view of the conference room door across the hall. "Call her a person of interest or a suspect or a witness. But in my book, she's at the top of the most-likely list even if you don't buy into my theory. In those papers is the preliminary criminal report I've pulled on her, along with her credit report."

"Have you read it yet?"

The chief shook his head. "Nope. I've been fielding phone calls from everyone in town from the mayor to the editor of the *Gazette*." With that, he once more propped his feet on the credenza, turning his back on Wade. "When you talk to her, I suggest you go in armed with the facts."

"You said something about a couple of interesting phone calls. Johansen and who else?"

"A guy who didn't want to leave his name, but who says he knows for sure that Megan Burke held a grudge against Robby Russell."

"He didn't leave his name," Wade repeated flatly.

"No. Caller ID was blocked, but we've got the phone company on it. I'll be sure to let you know when we hear something."

Wade nodded.

"Close the door behind you," the chief instructed as Wade left the room.

He discovered the door to the conference room was locked when he tried the knob. Nothing like making a witness even more nervous by locking her up, Wade thought. Unlocking the door, he pushed it open.

"Sorry you've had to wait all this time," he said, meaning it. This close, he could see her expression was drawn, her eyes red-rimmed. "Is there anything I can get for you? Coffee, something to eat?"

She shook her head, brushing her hair away from

her face. He remembered her hair had been in a ponytail this morning. Now it fell to her shoulders, softly curling around her neck.

"The ladies' room is back there. I've got one thing to do, which should take me no more than ten minutes."

She nodded her understanding, stood, and came toward him. Despite her height, she seemed fragile as she slipped past him, heading for the restroom. The urge to protect her overwhelmed him for a moment—and then he looked down at the papers in his hand.

Sitting down, he scanned Egan's notes and the record Caroline had printed. Megan was originally from New Jersey and evidently had come to Colorado to go to graduate school. She had worked as a physical therapist for several years in Denver at a rehab clinic affiliated with Denver General Hospital. Three years ago, she had moved here.

Three things stood out, and they were biggies. First, she had close to two hundred thousand dollars in savings—a lot of money for anyone, but a huge amount for someone on her wages. Second, she had changed her last name from Norris to Burke shortly after turning twenty-one. And third, she had been arrested and charged with assault and attempted murder.

He closed the file and stared down the hallway that led to the restrooms. He had been so sure she was one of the innocent ones. That, after telling Egan he didn't make assumptions.

Expelling a harsh breath of irritation at himself, he put everything inside a folder and waited for her return. One minute turned into two, and with each passing one, his level of irritation with himself and her grew. When she finally came down the hallway, the five minutes had felt like an hour. Her hair was once more in a ponytail, her expression more composed than it had been a few minutes earlier. He followed her into the conference room. She sat down, folding her hands neatly on the table, her gaze not quite meeting his. For some reason, that pierced his control.

He let the door slam behind him when he came into the room. She jumped slightly, but nothing in her expression changed when he sat down across from her.

"Tell me about Megan Norris," he said. "Tell me about your arrest."

She blinked, then something in her expression dissolved. There was simply no other word for it. In a matter seconds, color drained out of her face, leaving a white line around her mouth and making the freckles sprinkled over her nose stand out. She stared at him without speaking, but the expression in her eyes was so devastated that he imagined he was looking at a person in shock. He'd interviewed enough witnesses, suspects and victims over the last fifteen years to know when a reaction was faked, and when one wasn't. This was as real as it got.

The tug of sympathy pulled at his chest once more while he reminded himself he had a job to do. Collect the facts, build a case. Forget that he wanted to like this woman. That he already *did* like her.

"Did you read the whole report?" she asked, her voice surprisingly calm. "Or did you simply stop when you saw that I had been arrested?"

The fact that she seemed to know that further irritated him. "I want *you* to tell me about it."

She lifted her chin slightly. "We don't always get what we want, Detective. If you want the story…" Her voice trailed off and she swallowed, all the time holding his gaze as though he had somehow betrayed her. "Read the rest of the report."

"And then you'll talk to me about it."

She nodded, the reluctance in the gesture as obvious as her tightly clasped hands.

"Fair enough. Tell me about your relationship with Mrs. Russell," he said.

She did, her color improving little by little. They

were neighbors and friends. Everything she told him echoed what Helen Russell had told him when they had talked. Mrs. Russell had described how Megan watched out for her, shoveling the snow in winter, taking her to church and the grocery store. She'd never asked for anything, which contradicted the chief's theory that she was a gold digger. Megan's tone of voice and demeanor suggested that she genuinely liked her neighbor. But the knowledge that she had been arrested for attempted murder colored his perceptions, as unprofessional as that was. The cynic in him kept searching for motive in everything she relayed, but the side of him that wasn't a cop kept wanting to take what she said at face value.

When Megan fell silent, he said, "But you didn't like her grandson."

"I didn't," she agreed without any defensiveness in her voice. "Helen raised him, you know. So, I think it hurt her that he didn't visit very often. When he showed up a couple of weeks ago needing a place to stay, she was surprised."

Megan paused while she continued to study the detective. Common sense urged her not to volunteer anything. And the promise that she'd made to herself to live an open life after her father died last year was right there at the surface, too. Was it better, she wondered, to tell everything she suspected about Robby? Or was it better to operate the way she knew a lawyer would advise—keep her mouth shut. And if she did, would that make finding Robby's killer harder? And if she spoke up, would Detective Prescott assume he could—and should— build a case against her?

And then she remembered a verse from her Bible-study group a couple of weeks ago. *You will come to know the truth, and the truth shall set you free.* It had been true for her all those years ago when the finger of suspicion had been pointed at her. It *had* to apply now.

"I need to tell you about two different things that happened."

"Either of these come under the heading of your needing a lawyer?"

The question surprised her since her impression was that cops wanted information any way they could get it. Once more reminding herself that the truth couldn't hurt her, she said, "I'll take my chances. The first has to do with a strange thing that started about a month ago after a visit to the bank."

"Was that before or after Russell came to town?"

"Before, by a week or so," she replied. "Helen has this huge collection of old coins that she decided to have appraised. They were in a safety-deposit box at the bank, and she wanted help carrying them home."

"They were that heavy?" His soft question was interested, the kind friends asked when they were getting acquainted.

Ignoring the warning in her head that this man wasn't a friend, couldn't be a friend, she said, "You have no idea. She kept them in a washtub." Visualizing the plastic container, she motioned with her hands. "You know, like you'd set in the bottom of a sink. Anyway, we got them home, and she asked me to put them away on a shelf in the closet of her spare bedroom. A couple of days ago, she told me that the appraiser was finally coming to see her and asked me to get them down. At least a quarter of them were gone." She paused, the sick feeling in the pit of her stomach from that day back now.

"These coins...just how old are we talking?" Wade asked.

"Pre-civil war for a lot of the collection."

"And Mrs. Russell showed them to you."

"She did," Megan said. "Her father had begun the collection, and she had a story to go with many of the coins."

"And you think this has something to do with Robby's death?"

She met his gaze. "I don't know. It just seems

strange, you know?" She sighed. "The second part of this…Robby accused me of stealing from her."

"Were you?" The question so calm, so much still like two friends talking. Even so, her heart pounded.

"No. I wouldn't do that." She clasped her hands on top of the table, mentally repeating, *the truth will set you free.*

"So, you're telling me you're not a gold digger."

"Good grief, what do you take me for?" She stared at him, seeing an attractive man with penetrating brown eyes and a half smile. His posture was relaxed, an ankle drawn over the opposite knee, everything in his demeanor open. Friendly. Not at all like his stern-faced boss.

And yet, there was the accusation. The motive they thought she had, she realized. Swallowing, she looked away from the eyes that she had taken for kind.

"What's the second thing?" he asked. She must have given him a blank look because he tacked on, "You said you had two things to tell me. Missing coins and…"

"When Robby showed up a couple of weeks ago, he complained about being broke. Then, a few days after he got here, he wasn't, and he flaunted it."

"And?"

"I think *he* was stealing from Helen." She paused

and looked away for a second, too aware of Wade's focused energy directed at her. "Helen mentioned that she had misplaced a bracelet she often wore— a gold bangle. I'm talking real gold, not some piece of costume jewelry."

"And that's when you confronted Robby?"

Megan shook her head. "Not then. I didn't even make the connection until a few days later. Lou Gessner, the woman who owns the pawnshop, is in my Bible-study group. I asked her if she ever had any bangle bracelets, and she said one had just come into her shop a few days earlier. Then, the following Saturday morning, I saw him coming out of the pawnshop holding his money."

"Are you accusing this woman of accepting stolen goods?"

"Of course not," she said in defense of her friend, who was one of the most honest, forthright people she knew. "How is she supposed to know until she hears back from the police after she submits her reports?"

"Sounds like you know a lot about it."

"That's because I asked her," Megan said evenly, despite the accusation that once more laced Detective Prescott's voice.

"And that morning—what day was that?"

"Last Saturday."

"And you confronted him?"

"I did." Megan felt her throat close as she remembered those moments, now wishing they had never happened. "We got into it, and to be honest, I don't remember exactly what I said to him, but I do remember telling him that he was a thief and he didn't deserve to be Helen's grandson…and that she would be better off without him. Mr. Johansen saw us, and I'm sure he'll tell you pretty much the same thing if you ask him."

"You do realize what you're telling me, don't you?"

Megan opened her mouth to speak, then stopped when the detective held up his hand.

"If Johansen corroborates your story and says that you threatened Robby Russell…" His eyes bore into hers, and something there softened imperceptibly. "You need a lawyer."

She nodded her head. "Is this the part where you tell me that I'm a suspect?"

"Yeah." His voice turned gravelly. "At the moment, you're my only suspect."

FOUR

You're my only suspect. The statement was at odds with Wade Prescott's gentle expression she kept seeing in his eyes, despite his tough demeanor.

Megan had weighed the risks before deciding to be so open, and she really had believed this would all be okay. This was all so surreal that the urge to laugh bubbled up when Megan remembered how she had felt this morning when she had first walked out of her house. This was to have been a perfect day. It had all the ingredients—crisp autumn weather, a patient who was progressing well under her care, a life that pleased her. She had an equal urge to cry over how the day had turned out. Unfair as all this was, the day had been a far worse one for Helen Russell, a thought that burned behind Megan's eyes.

She met Wade's gaze, which had softened. She

really wished he'd stop looking at her that way because it made her want to like him.

"Are we done, then?"

He nodded without speaking.

"No advice to stay in town, keep my nose clean,
yada, yada?" She was being too flip, she knew, but
she couldn't help herself.

"Stay in town," he said, his voice still gravelly.
He cleared his throat. "Keep your nose clean." The
corner of his mouth lifted in an all-too-appealing
smile. "Yada, yada."

He looked away as though he, too, knew a
boundary had been crossed. A second later, he held
out a business card. She took it.

"You can reach me twenty-four hours a day," he
said. "Call me if…"

If what, she wondered, since she was no longer
a witness and talking to him without an attorney
wouldn't be wise. That was another thing. Finding
an attorney. Even though Natchez was the county
seat, theirs was a small community, and she was
pretty sure the half-dozen or so attorneys she knew
about lacked the skills and experience for the kind
of trouble she was in.

He raked his fingers through his dark hair that
immediately fell again over his forehead. "Let me
get one of the officers to take you home."

She stood. "It's all of seven blocks. I'd rather walk."

"I can understand that." He extended a hand as if waiting for her to take it. When she didn't, he put it his pocket in that do-not-touch gesture she remembered from this morning. "I'm sorry you waited so long."

It wasn't okay, so the normal response to an apology remained stuck in her throat. He opened the door, and she walked through it. She was acutely aware of his gaze on her as she headed through the empty front room of the police station. When she walked through the heavy door to the outside, she took in another deep breath.

Outside, the light was bright and the sky overhead was still a brilliant blue with only a few puffy clouds overhead. She thought about heading for home, but instead turned the opposite direction toward the offices for Our Daily Bread.

Halfway there, she began to shiver, despite the warm sunshine. She knew it was an adrenaline rush and would pass, but still had the overwhelming urge to run until her lungs burned. Her whispered prayer of thanks that she hadn't been formally charged or arrested failed to bring her any sense of peace.

When she pushed open the door to her place of

employment, everything looked so normal that she had that instant of disconnect where everything so far today had to have been a bad dream.

Megan saw her supervisor, Sarah Moran, sitting at her desk. At the ding of the bell when the door closed behind Megan, she looked up.

She smiled and headed toward Megan.

"Are you okay?" Sarah hugged her, then stepped back studying her face. "Rumor has it that Chief Egan took you to the station and that you'd been arrested."

"Just a lot of questions. That's all." Somehow, she had to keep believing that's all it would be despite his clear belief that she had killed Robby.

"Praise God," Sarah said. "I've been worried, but as I'm always saying—"

"Don't go borrowing trouble," Megan said with her.

They chuckled, then Sarah asked, "Have you eaten?"

Megan shook her head. "I'm not hungry."

Sarah led the way toward her office, motioning Megan to sit. "I called all your patients for the rest of the day. Their reschedules are up on the computer. So your afternoon is free. Maybe you should go home and clear your head," Sarah suggested gently.

Megan knew herself well enough to know that she'd spend the time dwelling on all of the "could haves" and "should haves," which wouldn't help her emotional state at all. "I think I'd rather stay here and catch up on my charts. At least for a while. I need to make sure Helen isn't alone—"

"She's not. Fiona Kassell is with her. And I called Reverend Ford—his wife said he'd been called earlier and was already there."

"That's good." Knowing that Helen was being cared for lifted some of the worry from Megan's shoulders, and she stood. "She has what she needs."

"I'm not sure you do." Sarah came around the corner of the desk, once more putting an arm around Megan. "I don't know what to do to help you."

"You already have. I'm fine." With that, she headed for the cupboard with her name on it. She went to work updating the charts and making notations in the computer, deliberately keeping her focus narrowed to the task at hand.

There was a certain level of peace that came with doing the monotonous job, knowing that she could control this. She'd been sure she was far enough behind that getting caught up would take her the rest of the day. It didn't, though. Which meant that sooner or later, she would have to go home.

She'd been through this before—returning to the scene of a violent death. And the truth was, she didn't want to do it.

"Go home," Sarah said to her as she came by the long counter that served as work stations for the staff. "You've been staring into space for the last ten minutes."

"Soon." Megan shut down the computer and pulled the files she needed for her appointments the next day.

"This was a big, traumatic deal today," Sarah told her. "If you need some personal time…"

"I don't."

"You'll ask if you change your mind?"

Megan knew she wouldn't be asking, but agreeing that she would was the path of least resistance, so she took it.

When she came outside ten minutes later, late-afternoon shadows were beginning to stretch toward the east.

Her steps lagged when she turned onto the side street that intersected with the one where she lived. At the corner, she could see the crime-scene tape still blocking off part of Helen's driveway and her own. Beyond that everything looked so ordinary. Nothing was left behind of the activity, which meant someone had been by to clean up the litter that inevitably came with having paramedics around. Not that they'd been able to help.

Someone getting out of a car across the street caught her attention. She recognized him—a friend of Robby's. Helen had introduced her to him at the bank once when Megan had driven her there.

"Ms. Burke?" he said, approaching her.

"Megan, please," she said, extending her hand. "I'm sorry, I've forgotten your name."

"Neil Dillon."

"I heard you were the one who found him. Are you okay? That must have been a serious shock," he said.

"I'm mostly worried about Helen. I was just going to check on her."

Megan looked over at Helen's house. The cat was sitting at its usual spot in the window, but it didn't look as though Helen was home. Neil looked in that direction, as well, his hands in his pockets, shifting from one foot to another.

"Helen told me once that you and Robby had been friends since grade school," Megan said.

He shrugged, his head bowed. "We have a lot of history together, that's for sure. I still can't believe—"

A car came to a screeching halt in front of her driveway. Jan Torrez, one of the partners that pub-

lished the weekly *Gazette,* came striding toward
them, her short brown hair looking messed as it per-
petually did, her glasses in their usual perch atop her
hair.

"You're a hard woman to catch up with," she said
as though they were close friends when, in fact, they
spoke only in passing. "How have you been? Well,
not today, of course, which was awful, just awful.
But otherwise." Before Megan could answer, she'd
whipped out a steno pad and pen, adding, "With a
story this big, Marty and I decided to do a special
edition. So, you were the one who found poor
Helen's grandson this morning. What time was
that?"

"I—"

"Don't remember? That's okay. I can see what
time the call came in to dispatch." She jotted a note
on her pad, then looked back expectantly at Megan.
"Did you know right away that he was dead or did
you administer CPR?"

"CPR." She closed her eyes for a moment as the
images from this morning assaulted her mind.
When she opened her eyes, Neil was headed back
toward his car, looking over his shoulder at Helen's
house as though he wanted to ring the doorbell but
couldn't quite face it.

"That must have been so hard for you, finding

someone murdered like that. Can you tell me what happened?" Jan pawed through the large bag that hung over her shoulder, digging out a tape recorder. "You don't mind if I record this, do you?"

"Actually, I think you should talk to the police." Megan pulled her keys out of her pocket and took a backward step toward her front door.

Jan's smile faded. "You don't want to give me a statement?"

"No, I don't. It's been a very long, stressful day. I'm sure you understand."

Jan clicked off the recorder and dropped it back in her bag. "You know how this is going to look, don't you? Like you have something to hide."

"I'm sorry." Megan headed for her front door, breathing a sigh of relief when she was able to slip inside and close it behind her. A moment later, she heard the car drive away. A look through the front window confirmed that Jan was gone. Neil Dillon sat in his car across the street, staring blankly out the window. Megan wished she had it in her to offer him some comfort, but she was spent. A moment later he, too, drove away.

She went to the kitchen and turned on the faucet, running the cold water for a second, then filling a glass. She drank, staring out the window, at a loss to remember what her personal plans had been for the rest of the day. Instead, her thoughts circled around Robby and the guilt she now felt over her active dislike of him, of wondering if she had seen or heard anything this morning that might have made a difference, of her sadness for Helen, who had already weathered so much loss in her life. Her husband, killed in the Second World War, her son, killed in Vietnam—and now her grandson. It was too much to contemplate.

Setting the empty glass in the drainer, she turned around, her tidy kitchen looking foreign somehow. The light was blinking on the answering machine, the display telling her that she had six messages. She stared at the display briefly, wondering if any of those messages were from Wade.

Stop thinking about the detective. A message from him would be bad news. And you've had enough of that for one day.

She decided that what she needed was physical activity to distract her from the forlorn thoughts circling through her head like vultures.

She grabbed a warm sweater out of the hall closet and went to the garage, then lifted her mountain bike from its rack on the wall. She had two hours before it was dark—enough time to ride out to Escalante Canyon and back. Enough time, hopefully, to burn off the excess adrenaline that made her hand shake and her mind latch on to worry after escalating worry.

She had just closed the garage door when she saw Fiona Kassell's old silver sedan pull into Helen's driveway. Fiona was so short, her dyed copper hair barely showed above the top of the steering wheel. Helen was in the passenger seat. As Fiona cut the engine, she was gesturing to Helen, who was shaking her head.

The unheard conversation continued as Megan left her bike and crossed the lawn. Helen spotted her and relief flooded her face. She opened the door, and Megan extended a hand to her friend.

"I've been worried about you," Megan said as she helped Helen out of the car. "Are you okay?"

"Oh, sweetie." Helen gave her a fierce hug, then held both her hands. "I've been so worried about *you*. Ever since Chief Egan took you away in his car and you didn't come back and didn't come back, I was afraid they'd gone and done something stupid like arrest you. And bless Caroline. That girl is good at her job—she wouldn't tell me anything even though I called four times." Helen stepped back, but didn't let go of Megan's hands.

"She couldn't," Megan said, watching Fiona come around the front of the car toward them. "Hi, Fiona."

"You tell me right now, young lady," Fiona demanded, the bracelets on her arm jangling as she pointed a perfectly manicured, age-spotted finger at Megan, "that the awful story Tom Johansen is telling all over town that you killed Robby is a bunch of nonsense."

"I...," Megan looked from Fiona to Helen.

"I know Megan," Helen said, "and she didn't kill Robby."

"Chief Egan didn't keep her at the station all this time because he likes her company," Fiona said.

"We just came from Hammond Mortuary," Helen added, ignoring her friend, "so things are ready when Robby's body is released. They took him to Grand Junction, you know."

Megan hadn't known, but she wasn't surprised since they didn't have a medical examiner here.

"Come have dinner with us," Helen said.

"She shouldn't do that." Fiona's gaze was as sharp as her tone. "Not until you know for sure that she's not going to be arrested for killing your grandson."

"Oh, stop it," Helen said, glaring at the woman who had been her best friend for more than forty years.

Megan gently squeezed Helen's hands and then kissed her cheek. "It's fine, Helen. I'm on my way out, anyway. I'll see you tomorrow?"

"Of course," Helen said. Megan was heading for her bike when Helen asked, "How was Glenna today?"

The reference to the patient that Megan was to have seen this morning made her throat tighten. She was reminded that nothing was normal or fine or right—and might not be for a long time.

"She can't tell you that," Fiona said briskly. "All those privacy laws and such."

"That's right," Megan agreed, her heart heavy for her friend.

She gave the two women a wave, ignoring Fiona's scowl, and retrieved her bike and headed down the street.

Within five minutes, she was at the edge of town and riding next to the orchards. Crates were stacked in intervals along the side of the road, a sure sign the red apples that glistened among the leaves would be picked within the next few days. A mile later, she turned onto a bike path that skirted another orchard before winding through scrub oak and piñon, whose wild, earthy scents were in stark contrast to the sweet fragrance of the ripening apples. The aromas calmed her thoughts. After riding another couple of miles, she took the path to her favorite spot: a wide slab of red sandstone overlooking the valley. She liked to sit here and pray.

She sank onto the rock, which was still warm from the sun's rays. She was comforted as she imagined God's presence surrounding her while she prayed for guidance, for peace of mind, for Helen during this time of grief, and for Robby's soul. Mostly she prayed for herself, that this overwhelming sense of fear and desolation would go away. She hated feeling this vulnerable, this alone, as she had been when she was eleven.

She closed her eyes and lifted her face to the warm rays of the setting sun. With effort, she reminded herself that God's love was ever present. Being thankful for that was always a good first step.

Reverend Ford had told her once that the potential for good flowed from every situation, no matter how tragic. What possible good could come out of today? She couldn't imagine. What if her reservoir of faith wasn't deep enough to see her through this?

The last rays of daylight faded. She knew she had stayed too long and that she'd be making the ride home in the dark. It was, she decided, a reminder that faith could illuminate even the darkest path.

FIVE

"What can you tell me about Robby Russell?" Wade asked the woman who had introduced herself as Mrs. Eve Harris when he knocked on her door Saturday afternoon.

She lived at the opposite end of the block from Helen and looked to be about the same age. He'd learned she'd lived here all her life, a fact she was supremely proud of.

"I've known him since he first came to live with Helen after his mother abandoned him. You've never seen a sadder little boy." She stepped onto her porch, folding her arms over her chest. "It's a shame what happened to him. When are you going to arrest that woman?"

"What woman?" he asked, even though he already knew. Each of the neighbors he'd talked to seemed to think that Megan had killed Robby.

"That Megan Burke, of course. She killed her sister, you know." Mrs. Harris shook a finger at him. "You've got one of those serial killers on your hands."

As had happened each time, his first impulse was to defend her as an innocent. The fact that Megan had been eleven when her sister died wasn't a part of the story that had made its rounds. So far, he hadn't figured out who was the source of the half-true story, so he didn't know if the motive behind it was the understandable worry that came from the current trauma or something more sinister. Like an attempt to frame an innocent woman.

"Had you talked to Robby since his return to town?" Wade asked.

"No. But I'm sure he'd have come around sooner or later."

"Why is that?"

Mrs. Harris stood a little straighter. "I make the best candy apples in the county, and that boy loved them."

"And Megan Burke—what makes you think she had anything to do with Robby's death?"

"Well, she was right there. Everyone saw her. And then there was the awful fight she had with him."

"And when was that?"

Mrs. Harris scowled. "I'm not sure. You know how time gets away from you."

"Did you happen to see this fight?"

"Well, no, but I heard all about it."

None of Megan's neighbors had actually seen the fight, but they were all more than happy to use it against her. And their retellings got more and more dramatic as the day went on. The fight had gone from a loud argument to a knock-down, drag-out brawl after which Robby had needed medical attention. So far, Wade hadn't found a bit of corroboration for that.

"And how has she been as a neighbor? Have you known her long?"

"She's a newcomer. You know, one of those people moving from the big city for the pleasures of our small community."

Wade nodded. "I'm new myself, so I can understand that. Anything unusual stand out about her activities?"

Mrs. Harris thought a moment, then shook her head. "She's quiet. And she rides her bike a lot. And if someone needs help, she's there to give a hand."

"Would you say she's a good neighbor?" he asked.

She scowled once more. "You don't think she killed poor Robby, do you?"

He closed his notebook and returned it to his

pocket. "Ma'am, I don't have enough evidence to have an opinion, yet." He handed Mrs. Harris his card, adding, "If you think of anything that might be relevant, you call me."

With a crisp nod, she retreated into the house, locking the screen door behind her.

As Wade headed for his car, his gaze went to Megan's house. It fit in with the others on the block— a small, tidy home with a front stoop and a well-kept front yard. But Megan herself was still considered an outsider, based on what he was hearing from the neighbors. Individually they were nice enough, but as a group they'd already tried and convicted Megan, despite considering her a good neighbor. In his experience, there was usually a ringleader in these situations. Someone with an ax to grind.

He wanted to know who, and he wanted to know why.

Fifteen minutes later, Wade walked through the door of Lou Gessner's pawnshop. Lou was one of the first people Wade had met when he moved here—in fact, he'd bought the nearly new grill on his patio from her. He was used to pawnbrokers being hard-nosed business people who cooperated because the law required them to, not because they thought doing so was right. In no way did Lou fit the typical mold, looking instead like someone's favorite aunt.

She looked up from the counter. "Hey, Wade," she said with a smile. She was of indefinable age, her skin smooth except for the smile lines around her eyes. She eyed the jewelry case that Wade was standing in front of. "I have a couple of nice pieces, if you're in the market."

"Not today. I'm here about Robby Russell."

"I figured you'd be around sooner or later," she said, going back to a desk tucked between a gun safe and a pair of ancient four-drawer file cabinets. "I wasn't sure whether this would have anything to do with that his death or not, but I pulled the tickets last night." She rummaged through one of the piles on her desk, then handed him the paperwork, including the reports she was required to file with the police that ensured she wasn't accepting stolen merchandise. "Give me a minute, and I'll get the jewelry out of the safe."

Something close to relief expanded through Wade's chest as he read through the tickets. Megan had been telling him the truth, at least about Robby's pawning jewelry—according to the ticket, a wedding ring, a fourteen-carat bangle bracelet and a pendant, the latter two pieces valued at a thousand dollars each. Until Helen made an identification, it remained to be seen if the items of jewelry on this list belonged to her.

"Did he say who these had belonged to?"

"Nothing that stands out," Lou replied, "except for the wedding ring. He said it had belonged to his father, and he had died in Vietnam."

"Not the sentimental type."

She laughed. "Him? No. He came in a couple of other times to pawn some old coins and a couple of firearms that date back to the Civil War era."

"But you didn't take them." Old coins again.

She shook her head. "His story didn't feel right. Plus, loaning on goods like that puts too much of my money in inventory that could take a long time to move." She looked back at the jewelry Robby had pawned. "I suppose you'll want that for evidence or something."

"That's right." Wade tagged each of the items and wrote out a receipt that he gave to Lou. "Those old coins—do you get much of that?"

She shook her head. "People with those kinds of collectibles either trade among themselves or go to dealers specializing in the stuff."

"Has Megan Burke ever pawned anything?" he asked.

Lou's eyebrows rose. "Is that an official question, Detective?"

He nodded. "Do you know her?"

"She's in my Bible-study group."

He hadn't had any reason to think Megan had lied about that, either, but he was glad for the confirmation. That put her at two for two, if he was counting. Maybe he was.

Lou shook her head. "You need to know that Megan is exactly what you see. And as for that stupid rumor, that girl no more killed Robby Russell than you did."

What-you-see-is-what-you-get isn't how he would have described Megan. He figured she was more like the layers of shale near his house, each one containing a possible surprise like the fossil he had found a few days ago.

"Wade, it doesn't take a rocket scientist to figure out what's going on here. Robby grew up in Natchez, so he's one of us. And Megan is new in town, relatively speaking, so she's an easy target. But she's the kind of person who would give you the shirt off her back if you needed it."

"A good neighbor?" He was too aware that he'd asked that question before. This need to have someone see Megan in the same light he did failed to make sense.

"Exactly. And this town's lucky to have a woman like her." Lou held Wade's gaze, a smile softening the glint in her eyes. "Now get out of here, Detective, so I can get back to work. Go protect and serve."

"Yes, ma'am," he replied, his light tone matching Lou's.

She laughed, and he headed out the door.

Lou's heartfelt defense of Megan kept running through Wade's head as he checked the air in the tires on his bike. If the woman's character was to be judged by the friends she had, Megan was in pretty good company.

When he'd moved here, he'd promised himself that he'd go mountain biking at least two or three times a week. So far, he'd only gone once.

He rode toward the edge of town with no particular destination in mind, his only intent to clear his mind. The wind against his face felt great, and he leaned into it, increasing his speed until his lungs began to burn. Only then did he ease off and take notice of his surroundings. He'd ridden past the last of the orchards toward the steeper roads at the edge of the valley.

He turned on to a well-used trail that took off away from the road and went along the edge of a ridge overlooking town. A few minutes later he pulled to a stop, took a drink of water and studied the view. It was one of the prettiest anywhere.

He took another sip of his water, enjoying the warmth of the late-afternoon sun against his face.

This sense of peace was what he'd wanted when he'd left Chicago. He knew too well the feeling was a fleeting one, and he longed to seize it, make it last.

That thought made it dissipate, and his mind was once more filled with the haunting images of Patty and Haley Lorenz, dead because he hadn't had enough evidence to keep their father in jail for assaulting them. Their father had come back, looking for their mother, and when he hadn't found her, he had beaten them to death. As bad as that memory was, the one that got him every time was the day their mother had been sentenced to a life term for killing him.

His faith to that point hadn't been something he thought about much—it was just there. But after that case, whatever faith he'd had in God was gone. The glimpses he had of God's presence, like looking at this beautiful sunset, were marred by the continuing violence people perpetrated against one another.

And here he was again, his gut instincts at odds with the preliminary evidence. Maybe the reason he was drawn to Megan was that she had survived an abusive father and deserved the life she had made herself. Maybe it was that he had an overwhelming sense she was telling him the truth. Maybe it was simply that she was a pretty woman and he liked her—he definitely wished he had met her some other way.

The sound of someone coming down the trail made him turn. His gaze lit on Megan Burke at the same moment she saw him. Her eyes widened in surprise, and he felt that now familiar punch in the middle of his chest. She came to a stop, indecision chasing away the surprise in her face. And, for the life of him, he couldn't imagine this woman as a killer.

"It's all right," he said, though he knew no such thing. "I was just on my way back to town."

She stood there, her legs straddling her bicycle, which was a lot like his. Unlike his, hers showed wear here and there, as though she rode often. He wondered if she belonged to the mountain-biking club he'd been intending to join all summer long.

"Really," he added, when she didn't say anything.

"I guess our paths are bound to cross," she agreed, pulling her water bottle from its holder on the frame of her bike.

"I kept thinking the same thing—wondered why we'd never met." The words were out even though he knew he shouldn't have admitted that to her. It sounded like a come on, though he hadn't intended it that way.

"Me, too." She took a swallow from the bottle before clipping it back in place.

Really? he thought, way too pleased with that notion.

"Do you come up here often?" When she looked at him, he couldn't decide if her expression was suspicious or merely surprised. "I'm just curious. One rider to another."

She studied him another moment before nodding. "When the weather is good, I ride up here almost every day. There's a place a little farther up that you can't see from the trail, but it has a great view."

"That's where you were headed?"

She nodded again, getting onto her bike and coasting slowly past him.

"Will it bother you if I follow along?"

Another hesitation before she murmured, "It's okay."

Wade let her get a little ahead of him before he followed, making sure he didn't crowd her. There were six dozen reasons he should turn around and go in the other direction, but he continued to follow Megan purely because he liked being with her. He wasn't supposed to feel like this, not now, not with this particular woman. At the moment, though, there was no other woman for him.

No other woman.

He must have lost his ever-loving mind.

And he felt more alive than he had in a long time.

Ahead of him, Megan disappeared from view, and a second later he saw where she had turned off the trail and was riding toward a large slab of sandstone. A pair of fragrant piñon grew to one side, the trees entwined together where their roots disappeared into the rocky soil. Megan slipped off her bike and set it down. Without looking to see if he followed, she headed for the edge of the slab of stone and sank onto it.

Wade chose to sit a good ten feet from her. She appeared to be praying.

In the same way that he hadn't given his own faith any thought, he'd never considered that of other people. Today, though, he wondered. How could Megan believe in some higher power, given what had happened to her as a child? And now, when her neighbors had turned on her and her future was uncertain at best, how could she be praying? He had no doubt that she was. This was no lament, begging God to spare her—her face was too serene for that, as though she had some unshakable certainty that…what? he wondered. That she'd be okay? He knew too well that might not be the case.

Whatever it was, he was surprised at how much he would give to have even a tiny bit of that for himself.

He was so lost in his own thoughts that Megan's voice seemed to come from a dream. "What do you see?" she asked.

He pointed toward the far side of town where a church steeple could be seen. "I live a block west of St. Paul's Church. I'm a little surprised that I can see the blue spruce tree in my neighbor's yard from here."

"You mean, the one over at the far edge of town?"

"That's right."

Her gaze turned to him. "Then you live next door to Reverend Ford."

"I do." The irony of his living next door to a pastor at this time in his life was not lost on him. They were silent awhile longer, and then Wade asked, "What do you think about the whole small-town thing, compared to living in a city?"

"You mean, running into your neighbors and co-workers in the grocery store, and everybody knowing everybody else's business?" She smiled. It nearly took the air out of his lungs.

"Among other things." He stared, too aware that he was wanting this moment to last way too much.

"I came here because I didn't want to be invisible anymore." She pulled her knees to her chest, resting her chin on her folded arms. "I guess I got my wish, huh?"

"But being visible isn't the same as being an insider, is it?"

"Not even close." Another long silence, and then she added, "My dad was released from prison while I was in college. Seven years for killing my sister."

"Not much time for a murder."

Closing her eyes as if against painful memories, she shook her head slightly. "He was convicted of manslaughter." She opened her eyes and looked at Wade.

He had the feeling of watching a fragile flower unfold, the tender petals susceptible to even a single drop of rain.

"Nobody who ever met him could believe he was capable of hurting—killing—anyone. He was polite, quiet, well dressed."

"Not the sort of monster who makes the evening news."

"No." She shrugged, the dismissive gesture at odds with the twisting of her hands, which she once more clasped around her knees. "But I knew…"

"Knew what?" he asked after a moment's silence.

She looked at him then, her blue eyes direct. "I've heard the talk, Detective, and I know what they're saying. Anyone who would believe I could kill Robby over money doesn't know me at all."

"Everybody seems to have a theory. What's yours?"

"I don't have one." Her gaze was steady while she met his. "Just a prayer."

She didn't offer it up, and so he asked, "Which is?"

"That you'll find the truth. It's the only thing that will set me free."

That surprised him. He'd been so caught up for years in seeking justice, he hadn't thought about truth even though he regularly made the vow that his testimony was the truth, nothing but the truth, so help him God. Wishing now that he had sat closer to her so he could reach out and brush the soft strand of hair away from her cheek, he said, "I hope I do, too, Megan."

SIX

"You're looking sharp this morning, Detective," said Caroline from the dispatcher's desk on Wednesday morning. "Court date today?"

For an instant, Wade heard only the word *date* and did a double take. Dates—as in dating Megan Burke and the impossibility of it—had been too much on his mind since his encounter with her last Saturday night.

"Funeral." He headed for his desk where he hoped he'd find the preliminary report from forensics today. He needed to know whose fingerprints were on that shovel—and whose blood. And if he was lucky, maybe the report would even turn up something unexpected. Imagine that.

He logged on to the computer, then went to snag a cup of coffee from the break room.

"Prescott," Chief Egan called from his office.

Wade stopped in front of his doorway.

"Are we any closer to having a suspect we can arrest? Folks are beginning to clamor, and we're running pretty far behind the local rumor mill." He pointed at the newspaper on his desk to emphasize the point.

"No closer." Wade had also read the article that suggested maybe the Natchez Police Department was outclassed for this big a case since an arrest hadn't been made yet.

"Still waiting on that forensics report, Chief."

"No probable cause for Ms. Burke yet?"

"Nothing even close," Wade said. "According to her, the money in her bank account came from a life-insurance policy when her father died. I'm going to verify that today. It seems there's no record she's ever touched the money. The car she drives was left to her last year by one of her patients after he died."

"Any chance she was involved in *his* death?"

"Not according to the man's daughter. Megan got to know him after he had a stroke, and he didn't like the idea of her driving around the county in an old rattletrap—the daughter's words, not mine—and wanted her to have reliable wheels. She said Megan was very kind to her dad and that she had the family's eternal gratitude."

"Nobody can be that perfect," the chief said. "Keep digging. What about the old coins you found?"

"That's one of several things to talk to Helen Russell about, which I hope to do today after the funeral or tomorrow."

The chief picked up one of the copies of the reports that Wade had been turning in every night. "Never heard of such a thing as a half-dime."

"Evidently they were common before the Civil War. I don't have the appraisal back, but according to my preliminary information these are worth anywhere from fifty or sixty dollars each to several thousand."

"Each?" Chief Egan whistled. "That's a huge range."

"It all depends on their condition and rarity."

"Let's hope this leads to something. Find your man—or woman—and make the arrest."

Wade glanced at his watch. "I'm hoping for a few more leads at the funeral this morning."

"You think the murderer will be in attendance?"

"It wouldn't be the first time," Wade said. "I'll keep you posted."

Wade returned to his desk, checked his e-mail and found the report from the forensics lab. The garden spade was most likely what had been used to hit the victim over the head. They'd pulled fingerprints and only two sets were identifiable: the victim's and Megan Burke's. It would be weeks before they had DNA evidence back on the blood, but two types had been found on the handle, only one matching Robby Russell's. The other was B positive.

He'd hoped that the placement of Megan's fingerprints on the handle would clear her of the crime. They didn't. His heart sank as he studied the accompanying photographs of the prints. The pattern could indicate she'd picked up the spade to get it out of the way before administering CPR. It could also indicate she'd used the shovel as a club.

Wade closed the e-mail and headed out the door. He was on the way to the funeral when Megan's voice began to replay in his head. *Anyone who would believe I could kill Robby over money doesn't know me at all.* What if something else had been the motive? He really hated this cold stone in the middle of his stomach that had him wishing she'd denied she could kill for any reason. Except, he knew that wasn't the truth. Push hard enough on the right raw spot, and anyone was capable of murder.

When he pulled into the parking lot of St. Paul's Church, he was surprised to find it nearly full.

Equally surprising was that Helen Russell stood outside, greeting people as they came in. In his experience, the bereaved clustered in a secluded spot until services began. Helen stood tall, though, firmly taking the hands of those who had come to pay their respects and speaking with each person. She'd been as steady as a rock the day of the murder, and it looked as though today was no different.

Megan Burke stood on one side of her, and an old lady with copper-colored hair stood on the other. Wade assumed this was Fiona Kassel. She'd been so firm with him over the weekend, refusing to allow him to talk to Mrs. Russell, that he'd expected her to be six feet tall, not an inch or two shy of five feet. His attention turned to Megan. There it was again, that surprising nudge of interest that he never expected. Today, it competed with his disappointment in her over the evidence found on the garden spade.

Compared to the two older women, she was a beacon, not only for her height but for her shiny, sun-streaked hair. She wore it down today and it shimmered as she moved. Even from where he stood, a good twenty-five feet away from her, there was no hiding her vivid eyes. He knew the second her gaze lit on him, and he headed toward the end of the receiving line.

"Oh, Detective," Helen said when he moved into

her line of vision. "How nice of you to come." She clasped his hand, and he had the feeling she really meant it, which somehow made a mockery of his business reasons for being here.

At her side, one of Megan's eyebrows rose slightly, signaling to Wade that she knew as well as he this wasn't a social call.

Still, she was polite when she introduced the other woman at her side, "Fiona, this is Detective Prescott. Detective, this is Helen's good friend, Fiona Kassel."

"We've spoken." Fiona's handshake and firm voice would have been just right on a five-star general. "You're new here."

"Yes, ma'am." Wade had the feeling that, in Fiona's eyes, he'd still be "new" ten years from now.

"You're that hotshot detective that Chief Egan went and hired." That sounded like an accusation, even more so after she added, "Nothing in the paper yet about you making an arrest."

"No, ma'am."

Her gaze shifted to Megan. "Are you going to arrest her?"

Megan flushed while Wade analyzed the tone in Fiona's voice. He couldn't decide what her agenda might be.

"Any reason I should?"

"Humph." She looked him up and down once more. "You best be getting to work, then, if you don't have enough evidence to arrest someone."

"My chief agrees with you."

"Smart man," Fiona said while Helen reached for his hand, patting it and saying, "Let the boy be. I'm glad you came to pay your respects to my grandson."

"Helen, I think it's time we went inside," Megan said.

Helen straightened her shoulders. "I guess we can't put this off any longer, can we?" A slight tremor in her voice was the only crack in her armor that Wade had noticed.

Wade offered Helen his arm. Head held high with dignity, she took it, and all four of them moved into the church and down the aisle.

While they moved toward the front of the church, Wade found a place near the back. His neighbor, Reverend Kyle Ford, stood at the front of the church next to the casket, his glance catching Wade's as he sat down. The reverend had invited him here, of course, but hadn't pressed when he'd made excuses.

This was the first time he'd been in church in a long time, and he sat there remembering the other times. Funerals like this one where he was working, looking for clues. Funerals like the one for Patty and Haley Lorenz where the grief of their mother flayed him.

Wade took a breath, and somehow a stillness… peace…settled over him, something he hadn't felt since he was a boy. The idea that he might have peace now…here…in the midst of another murder investigation…had him raising his head in denial.

"'Incline your ear, and come to me,'" Reverend Ford began. "'Hear, and your soul may live.' Let us pray."

Odd as he found it, Wade did, for the first time since he'd been a boy, caught in his memory of watching Megan pray yesterday afternoon and lacking the courage to ask her about it. As soon as the "amen" came, he lifted his head, his senses unerringly finding her.

He'd come here looking for a killer, but instead he watched Megan. Through the entire service he had the feeling she was Helen's anchor and that she would do whatever was required to support her friend.

An hour later, Wade leaned against the side of his car, watching the last of the mourners leave the grave site. The cemetery was at the edge of town in a picturesque spot surrounded by apple orchards, with a view of Grand Mesa's wooded slopes to the east. Like the funeral, the graveside service had been simple and heartfelt. But the peace Wade had felt during the services faded, and his focus returned to the investigation.

To his irritation, no one had stood out as someone with motive of any kind, much less enough to commit murder. The people in attendance had included Helen's neighbors and friends from around town, who came from all walks of life. There had been a surreptitious glance or two sent his way, but Wade figured that was more about his being a cop than anyone having something to hide.

Robby might have been a hometown boy and therefore held in some regard, but the man had few friends he'd stayed in touch with.

That thought had Wade thinking about the friends—or lack of them—that Robby Russell had. The ones who came and went with the jobs he'd had and hadn't stuck with. Except for the partner Wade had left behind in Chicago, his own friendships weren't that different than Robby's had been, a realization that made him internally squirm. Once more refocusing his attention, he watched the people beginning to leave the graveside.

A young man was earnestly talking to Helen, and the tension in Megan's body language had Wade taking a longer second look. The guy was dressed in a gray suit and bright blue shirt, the getup looking more like something he'd see worn by a lounge singer at a Chicago club than at a funeral, especially a small-town funeral. The guy moved away from the women, sunlight glinting off his patent leather shoes. His gaze skipped over Wade, then came back. Something in his expression changed, and he headed toward Wade.

"You that detective on the case?" he asked, coming to a halt a few feet shy of Wade's car.

"Yep." Wade held out his hand. "Wade Prescott. You're…?"

"Neil Dillon," he said, shaking Wade's hand. He looked back at the grave site where Helen was surrounded by her two friends and Reverend Ford. "Robby and I…we went to school together."

"Had you seen him since he came back to town?"

"Not much. A couple of times, I guess." He straightened his tie, then shifted from one foot to another. Everything in the man's body language suggested he was trying to figure out how to say whatever was on his mind.

"Because of my position at the bank…"

"What position is that?" Wade asked.

"Sorry, I work at the bank. I'm, uh, in the management-trainee program."

Wade nodded, waiting for Neil to continue.

"Anyway, I'm privy to certain information."

"Yeah," Wade agreed, hoping his tone sounded encouraging.

"Well, for example, I happen to know Mrs. Russell is a very wealthy woman. And Robby was going to inherit everything."

Wade waited, not indicating one way or the other whether he already had this information.

"And she's getting old—forgetful, if you know what I mean."

"I'm not sure I do," Wade said.

"She'd be easy for someone to take advantage of," Neil said, glancing at Megan.

"Do you mean someone like her neighbor?"

"I don't mean to point the finger, Detective. I really don't. I just think it might be good for you to know that Ms. Burke often brought Helen Russell to the bank, and she was there the day Mrs. Russell took this big collection of coins out of her safety-deposit box."

"When was this?" Wade asked.

"About a month ago," Neil said. "Ms. Burke was acting a little strange, like she didn't want Mrs. Russell talking about the coins."

"How well did you know Robby?"

"We went through school together, but he'd been

away for a long time. I can't really say that I knew him well anymore."

"Do you know of anyone who might have had a reason to kill him?"

Neil glanced at Wade and then looked away, shaking his head. "I don't. Poor Robby. What happened to him was…well, it's a tragedy."

"It almost always is when someone gets murdered," Wade said. "I'm sorry for your loss."

"Anyway," Neil said, "I just thought you should know. It might not be anything—"

"Did you ever see Megan and Robby arguing?"

"No. But everyone in town knew about the fight they had."

"And what fight was that?"

"The one where she accused him of pawning Mrs. Russell's jewelry. It happened in front of his store," Neil said, gesturing toward an elderly couple walking toward their car. Wade recognized Thomas Johansen.

"What about my store?" The pharmacist came to an abrupt halt, wild gray eyebrows drawn together.

Neil flushed. "I was, uh, just telling the detective about the fight in front of your store."

"The detective knows all about that, young man."

He gave Wade a curt nod and continued on his way.

"Anything else?" Wade asked Neil.

Neil shook his head. "I don't want to gossip."

Wade handed him a card. "Thanks for talking to me, Neil." He watched as Neil made his way to his car.

From her place where she stood between Helen and Pastor Kyle, Megan watched Wade while the last people at the grave site offered Helen their condolences. Personally, Megan didn't understand why they couldn't wait until they got to the house where the ladies from the church were setting out lunch. They'd be going through all this again. And the stress of it was beginning to wear on Helen.

That didn't keep Megan from wondering what Wade had found out, however. Clearly, he was working. She supposed it didn't take any great leap of imagination to think whomever killed Robby had come to the funeral. She shuddered at that thought. She knew most of these people. She'd known what it was like to have someone you knew be a murderer, and she had hoped she'd never be in that position again.

As if answering some silent summons, Wade met her gaze and came toward them. Fiona glowered at him and Reverend Ford smiled.

"I finally got you into church," he said, offering his hand and making Megan remember that Wade had told her they were neighbors.

"It was a nice service," Wade said, one of his rare smiles on his lips—this one almost reached his eyes. Almost. What would it take to make the man really smile? she wondered. Based on the reverend's comment, she guessed it wasn't church.

"Thank you for coming," Helen said, as she had repeatedly said to everyone all morning long.

"You're welcome," Wade answered.

"You're coming to the house?" Helen asked.

"Not this afternoon," he said. "But I would like to come talk to you tomorrow morning."

"That's fine," she said.

"Not too early, young man. Helen is going to be tired," Fiona added.

"I'm fine," she insisted.

"Shall we go?" Reverend Ford motioned toward the car from the funeral home, where a driver stood waiting.

"Megan," Wade said as the others headed for the vehicle.

She stopped and met his dark eyes, the expression there as close to uncertain as she'd seen on him.

"I have some additional questions. Can I drop by to see you later?"

She nodded, her heart thudding. She couldn't decide if it was because she wanted to see him again or was dreading it.

"About six this evening? Does that work for you?"

She nodded. "I'll see you then."

He walked away, turning once and catching her eyes. She would have sworn he was going to say something else, but he didn't. But something in his expression seemed like a warning. And she recognized the feeling in her chest.

Fear.

SEVEN

"I'll see you in a couple of days," Megan said to Glenna Adams, the stroke patient she'd been working with for the past month. "You're making such good progress that we may be able to cut back your PT to once a week."

"And miss all this torture you put me through?" Glenna said with a laugh, her words carefully pronounced. "I won't miss that, but I like having you come see me."

"After I talk to your doctor, I'll call you." Glenna's praise was confirmation that working for a few hours was preferable to being at home, wondering what Wade wanted to talk to her about. Detective Prescott, she reminded herself.

Since seeing him the other night, she was having a much harder time remembering that he was, first of all, the detective investigating Robby's death.

She had nothing to hide, but she also couldn't quite forget that he'd told her she was a suspect. The speculations from a couple of her neighbors had gone quite a bit beyond that.

"You look all lost in thought," Glenna said, "like you were a million miles away."

Megan shook her head and smiled at the older woman. "Sorry. It's just been a strange several days."

Glenna patted her hand. "You tell my old friend Helen that I'm praying for her, won't you."

"I will," she promised, saying her goodbyes and loading her gear into the car. Since it was nearly an hour's drive, she'd be cutting things close to be home in time to meet Wade.

Detective Prescott.

The sun was hanging low in the western sky— she was thankful to be driving east so she didn't have the glare in her windshield. Even better, Grand Mesa's ramparts would be laid out for her for most of the drive home.

As always on this particular drive, she was struck by how fine God's creation was. How thankful she was to live in the midst of all this beauty.

She'd been on the road maybe ten minutes when she noticed a car coming up rapidly behind her. She expected it to pass her, but it didn't, just hung behind her, matching her speed.

Over the next few miles, a couple of other cars came up behind them, and as soon as the road was clear, passed them. Something about the way the car followed her so closely raised the hair on the back of her neck. She slowed a little to see if the vehicle would come close enough for her to see who was driving. But it dropped back, and she couldn't see a single distinguishing thing about the driver.

She accelerated, exceeding the speed limit by five miles an hour. Then ten, then fifteen. And the car was right there, pacing itself at an even distance behind her.

Where is a state patrolman when you want one?

The sun dropped below the horizon, and the car's headlights came on, a pair of unblinking malignant eyes. She remembered feeling just like this once before, all tight and worried inside. Never mind she'd been a child then.

She had been with her sister, Ellen, who had just gotten her license. Ellen decided that picking Megan up from soccer practice was the perfect chance to take a detour to the pizza parlor so she could see the boy she liked, Jim Strahan.

"Just one little stop on the way home," Ellen had said to her. "It'll be fun, I promise."

Megan had been all sweaty from practice, which

made being Ellen's dorky little sister even worse. The pizza parlor had been crowded, and she'd hung around the kids playing arcade games while she'd watched Ellen flirt with Jim.

When they'd finally headed home that night, her sister had been all happy at first, and then she had seen something in the rearview mirror that had scared her. Megan turned around and saw only the headlights of a car behind them and the shadow of a hulking figure at the wheel.

Those headlights had followed them right into their driveway. It was their dad, and then he was out of his car, screaming about what a no-good tramp Ellen was, and how no daughter of his was going carry on like that.

He'd hit Ellen hard, right across the face, and Megan had run into the house, past her mother who was at the kitchen sink, scrubbing a pot like nothing was out of the ordinary. The worst part was, nothing was.

Two weeks later, Ellen was dead and her family was destroyed.

And though Megan knew her father could no longer hurt her, those headlights made her feel like he was right there, ready to pounce the moment she stopped. She wiped her sweaty palms on her pants.

Instead of feeling relief when she reached the

edge of town and the first of the streetlights, Megan imagined the vehicle following her right to her own driveway. A cold stab of fear ran down her spine.

When the police station came into view, she made a sudden decision and turned left into the parking lot next to it.

She looked up, and the car that had been following her drove right past, a sedan that looked like hundreds of others. She couldn't see the driver or the license plate or even the exact color of the car—it was too dark.

She dropped her head to the steering wheel. *Was I really in danger or have I just completely lost my mind?*

A sharp rap on the window took a year off her life.

Her head whipped up, and there was Wade, leaning down with concern etched on his face.

"Are you okay?" he asked through the window.

She nodded.

"What are you doing here?" he asked. "I thought we were meeting at your house."

She sucked in a shuddering breath. "I think someone was following me."

His eyes hardened and he raised his head to look at the street. "Did you recognize the car?"

"No. I couldn't even see it, really. The only thing

I can tell you is that it was a light-colored sedan that looks like most other cars."

"When did you first notice it?" he asked.

"About five minutes after I left my patient's house. Near the end of Granger Gulch Road."

"That's close to an hour away. Why didn't you call?"

She swallowed. "He could have been someone on the way to town."

"And that's what has you so jumpy. Some random car traveling the same direction you are."

He sounded indignant, as though her safety mattered to him at some personal level. Which was ridiculous, she decided, even as butterflies fluttered in her stomach at the thought.

"I wasn't sure. It could have been a coincidence. You know?"

"What I know is there are no coincidences." He grabbed her hand and urged her out of the car. "Come on."

"Where?" She pulled the keys from the ignition and stood next to him, sheltered somehow by his large frame and the car door. He stared at her a second, the hardness easing out of his eyes, and that half-lopsided smile melting her a little.

"I'm starving," he said, leading her away from the car. "And I figure this is going to take a while."

"What is?"

"You telling me about the lowlife following you."

"You want me to cry on your shoulder about something that may or may not even be true while you eat?"

He grinned. "I figure you'll feel better after you get something to eat, too."

"Weren't you supposed to be heading to my house? You said you wanted to talk to me."

"I do. Except right now, I'm starved."

"Okay." Eating with him almost made sense. Almost. His hand was warm and comforting. She liked holding it—too much. "You're off duty. Why don't I go home and you can—"

"I promise not to ask you anything about the case. And you can tell me why you're so spooked."

"I'm not," she said, pulling her hand from his.

"Yeah, sure." He tipped his head to the side. "It's just food, Megan."

She couldn't argue with that, though she knew she should at least try. "Okay," was the best she could come up with. So much for arguing. "I'm paying for my own dinner."

He laughed. "Now why did I know you were going to say that?"

Inside the diner, no one gave them a second

glance, and Megan breathed a sigh of relief as they were seated in a booth away from the busy counter. As she studied the menu, the words blurred together because all she could think about was that she was having dinner with Wade Prescott. Of all people.

She peeked at him over the top of the menu. His was already folded up and sitting at the edge of the table. And, he was watching her, his manner subtly different from the day he'd questioned her. She remembered thinking he was a hard-edged city cop. Maybe he was, but that wasn't how he seemed just now.

"You've already decided?" she asked.

"Yep." He smiled. "You want some help?"

"No, thanks, I can handle it." When the waitress returned, she ordered the daily special.

"Good choice," Wade said. "That's what I'm having, too."

"Copy cat," Megan said, and Wade laughed. Oh, what a laugh it was. Warm. Delicious. And she wanted to hear it again.

"Tell me about the car, Megan."

"Tenacious has nothing on you, does it?"

"My middle name," he agreed. "It's part of what makes me a good cop."

She stared out the window at the dark street. "It's probably nothing."

"That would be my preference," he said, "since I don't like the idea that someone might be stalking you."

That possibility made her throat close. She'd spent the years after her father was released from prison trying to be invisible, and the thought that she was on some crazy person's radar was close to unbearable. She related what she'd noticed about the car, details so thin she hated even saying anything.

"It's nothing," she finished just as their dinner was delivered.

"Maybe," he said. "But you should always pay attention to your instincts. Chances are good that your subconscious has latched on to something your conscious mind hasn't processed yet."

She didn't want to agree with him, because that meant she really might have something to worry about. Searching for a neutral topic, she said, "You mentioned the other night that you're digging up your backyard. Tell me about that."

"There's not much to tell." He reached for the basket of rolls. "At the moment, I have this patch of red dirt that grows nothing but bindweed. So every night when I get home, if it's not dark yet, I get the shovel out and turn over another row."

"Why don't you just get a rototiller and be done with it?"

"That's what Kyle Ford keeps asking me, too."

That was the end of any awkward silences as he told her about the hard clay of his backyard and his determination to plant trees and have a lawn. She laughed at his descriptions of the mud and his claim that building the Hoover Dam had been a smaller project. He also managed to get her to talk about herself a bit, and he expressed an interest in going mountain biking sometime with the group she belonged to. She liked that idea, too easily imagining how it would be.

The truth was, she liked this man. It was more and more difficult to remember the reasons they shouldn't be sitting here having a conversation like two friends. Like two adults beginning to be interested in each other. She'd dated enough to know when there was chemistry…and there was chemistry.

"What do you do to relax?" he asked, cutting into her thoughts. "Besides cycling."

"Pray," she said. She wasn't sure why she'd confessed that.

"And what do you pray for?" His gaze was earnest as though he really wanted to know.

"To notice my blessings, mostly."

"Even in a week like this one?"

She smiled. "Especially in a week like this one."

His expressive eyes darkened, and she wondered if the idea of praying had scared him off. Though she had long ago accepted that many people went through their lives without God as a daily presence, she couldn't imagine living her life like that. Maybe Wade found peace with his gardening project—his version of "haul wood and chop water." In her view, God was there, too, even if Wade hadn't realized it. Or simply didn't want to.

"You'll have to bundle up soon," she said, "if you continue turning over your garden after winter sets in."

"It can't be as bad as Chicago was," he said, his gaze shifting to something beyond her.

She turned around to see. Chief Egan was coming toward them, his ever-present frown deeper than ever.

"Detective, I need to speak with you."

"We're almost finished with dinner. Can I meet you at the station in about ten minutes?"

Wade's eyes had gone hard again, she noticed, though, his tone was conversational.

"Now." The chief turned around and marched toward the front door.

Wade wiped his mouth with his napkin and said, "I'll be right back. Excuse me."

She watched him go, noticing that others were

watching him, too. One of the drivers from Our Daily Bread was there with his wife, and he gave Megan a small wave—his wife did not. As the others turned back to their meals, her gaze strayed outside to Wade and Chief Egan.

The argument was clearly heated, the chief gesturing in her direction. Megan could only imagine how he'd seen this apparent fraternization between his detective and a suspect.

Her appetite gone, Megan reached for her purse and headed toward the cash register at the end of the counter.

"Chief Egan sure looks mad, doesn't he?" someone said.

Megan looked up and found Neil Dillon sitting at the counter, about halfway through his meal.

"Oh, hi, Neil. I didn't see you there."

"You doing okay?" he asked.

"I am, thanks."

"Good. Glad to hear it. I know there's an awful lot going on right now. A lot to deal with."

Megan handed her money to the cashier and looked out the window in time to see Chief Egan storming away. Wade was just standing there, hands on his hips.

"Ms. Burke—"

"I'm sorry, Neil, I have to go," she said, desperate to get away from the prying eyes of the other diners. What had she been thinking to agree to come here with Wade?

EIGHT

The chief strode toward the police station just as Megan came out the door, wearing the carefully blank expression of a person who didn't want to know what had just happened. Wade didn't blame her any, but he hated that she didn't look at him as she came out the door and headed away from him.

"Megan, wait," he called to her as she began walking toward her car. "I'll walk with you."

"And give your boss something more to give you grief about?"

"I'll live."

They walked in silence a moment, and he thrust his hands into his pockets to make sure he didn't take one of hers. That would just about cap it for the chief—to find the guy he'd just reprimanded for dating a suspect holding hands with her. As if Wade had ever dated a suspect. As if he ever would.

Wade stole a glance at Megan. In her case, he'd like to be dating her. What he'd told her about paying attention to your instincts was doubly true. She'd no more murdered Robby Russell than he had.

He knew it, despite the fingerprints on the shovel and the argument she'd had with the man.

Wade had enjoyed having dinner with her, and he wished it could have been a date, even though he'd promised himself to stop wishing for things he couldn't have.

"I don't get you," she said, sounding angry, as she came to a halt in the middle of the sidewalk. The police station parking lot was only fifty feet farther on.

He stopped and turned. "What's to get?"

She waved a flailing arm. "This. Us."

There was an us? Much as he liked that idea, she didn't look all that pleased. Okay, there wasn't supposed to be an "us." He wasn't supposed to be thinking this way, but he couldn't deny that he liked the idea.

"You make me crazy, you know that?" she said.

He opened his mouth to speak, not at all sure what might come out.

She saved him by rushing on, "One minute, I'm a suspect in a crime you're investigating, and the next you're asking me out—"

"I didn't ask you out," he defended. Chief Egan

had accused him of the same thing. He hadn't. That was his story and he was sticking to it. "That was dinner. Food. Just like I told you it was."

"And then you say things like you… Like we…" She turned around in a circle, wrapping her long sweater more tightly around herself.

This was getting interesting. Her color was high and that arm was flailing about again.

"Like you…" She swallowed and looked away. "Like you *like* me."

The last was said on a hoarse whisper that shocked the daylights out of him and seemed to surprise her, as well, because she clapped a hand over her mouth, her eyes wide.

The vulnerability in her expression made keeping his distance impossible. He stepped closer and pulled her hand away from her face, feeling the warmth of her breath on his own hand.

"I do like you," he admitted, wanting to lean over and kiss her. "Now, before that gets us in any trouble…" he gave her a gentle nudge in the direction of her car "…go home."

She took a couple of steps before turning around to look at him, her beautiful eyes all soft. "Good night, Wade."

Not trusting himself not to say something stupid, he simply waved.

So this, this…thing…wasn't one sided. Oh, Megan, he thought. Be as innocent of this whole mess as you seem. Please be innocent.

When Wade rang the bell at Helen Russell's Thursday morning, she opened it with a big smile. "Oh, good. You're just in time." She moved out of the doorway and motioned him in. "I'm so glad to see you. I was wondering how I was going to get all this loaded into my car. Megan will be here in a minute, but at the moment, you're an answer to a prayer."

Megan would be here in a minute? He'd checked her driveway when he'd arrived, and her car wasn't there.

He followed Helen through her house, which was filled with the aroma of apples. In the kitchen, he saw why. Dozens, possibly hundreds of apples had been peeled and placed on wooden skewers stuck in plastic-foam sheets. Not just apples, he realized, but carved faces. He picked one up and gave it a closer look, the drying apple revealing a surprisingly realistic face.

"Gives you a bit of a fright at first, doesn't it?" she said cheerfully.

The cheerful tone in her voice had him puzzled, too, as he took in all the carved heads. Now that he thought about it, he remembered seeing the apples the other day, but it hadn't sunk in then that they were carved heads.

"What is all this?" he asked.

"Step one of the Apple Dumpling Gang. It's our annual fund-raiser for the seniors' center. We have a booth at the Apple Festival in a couple of weeks."

"You sell these?"

Helen smiled. "Not like this. They all have to be dressed and accessorized. We're meeting this evening at the seniors' center to add the bodies and clothing."

"We?"

"Everybody who wants to pitches in," she said. "This was Megan's brainchild."

Wade looked around the kitchen. "Hate to tell you, Helen, but even if you drive a Humvee, I don't think all this will fit in your car."

"Which is why we're going to load mine *and* Megan's." She looked around the kitchen once more. "Good thing you came by. We might need to load some of these in your car, too."

He had a schedule to keep, but there was no stopping her, and she gave orders with more authority than a police captain. He followed her directions, carrying the plastic-foam sheets to her vintage Buick and carefully loading them in, the wizened faces appearing to watch him. The one trip between her car and the kitchen became several.

After they had loaded up Helen's car, she frowned, glancing over at Megan's house. "I don't understand what's happened to her. She said she'd be here as soon as she got off work."

Off work? Wade glanced at his watch. It wasn't even ten yet. "What time did you expect her?"

"She promised she'd be no later than five today."

He gave Helen a closer look. "Five this afternoon?"

"That's right," she said as though he had asked a foolish question.

"Mrs. Russell, what time does your watch say?"

She looked down, studying her watch for a long moment. "Well, that can't be right," she told him. "My watch says nine-forty-five."

Wade held up his arm, pointing at his own. "That's what mine says, too."

"Oh." Her shoulders slumped and she shook her head. "If that's not the strangest thing… I was positive it was Thursday afternoon."

It had to be the stress of losing her grandson. "It's morning, Helen," he said gently.

"It is?" She stared at him a moment, her expression completely perplexed. "Well, my goodness. This just makes no sense, does it?" She looked at her car. "And you were so nice to help me."

"It was no problem." Helping was no problem, but this memory lapse was potentially a big one, and he wondered if her confusion was due to the stress of her grandson's death or some stage of Alzheimer's. "Are you a coffee drinker, Mrs. Russell?"

"Yes."

"I'd love a cup, if it's not too much trouble." Wade figured doing something ordinary was the ticket to making Helen feel more like herself before he brought up the subject of the pawned jewelry that was in the pocket of his jacket.

She smiled. "Let's go see if there's some in the pot, since it's still morning and all." Her tone was cheerful, but her smile was strained. He wasn't looking forward to causing her more stress by asking her questions about Robby's activities.

Sure enough, there was coffee in the coffee-maker, and it was still warm.

"Well, I can tell you that's a relief." She took down a couple of mugs. "I sure never thought I'd be one of those dithering old women who lose track of the time. I must tell you, I feel very foolish."

"It could happen to anyone," he said. "After all, you've had a pretty stressful week."

She frowned as she sat at the table across from him. A cat wandered into the room and rubbed against her legs.

"Funerals are never easy, and this one had to be especially difficult," he said.

She stared out the window a moment, her confused expression easing a bit. "I never expected I'd be burying my son."

"No, I don't suppose you did." Wade wondered if she had intended to say "grandson."

"Why did you come see me?" she asked.

He pulled the evidence bags from his pocket and set them on the table. "I wondered if you might recognize these things."

She picked up the bag with the wedding ring first.

"Go ahead and take it out," he said. She pulled on the seal, the ring falling into her hand. She ran the tip of her finger over the outside, then the inside as if feeling for a design or an engraving. There were intricate knots etched on the outside of the band.

"I haven't seen this in a long time," she said.

"So it's yours?"

She shook her head. "My husband's." Her eyes grew soft. "The last day he was home, we traded. I wore this on a chain around my neck and he had mine with his dog tags. In some ways, it seems like yesterday, instead of a whole lifetime ago."

She slipped the ring, which was many sizes too big, on her finger, watching the play of light over the gold as she turned her hand this way and that. "There's an inscription that reads 'They two shall be one flesh.' We'd been married only three years when he died." She stared out the window again, her gaze unfocused. A moment later she added, "That was July 23, 1944. I was five months pregnant with our son."

Wade watched her steadily without saying anything, feeling like an intruder on her private, wistful memories.

A moment later, she began telling him about the early days without her husband and her worry about being a good parent.

"Did you remarry?" Wade asked when her voice trailed off.

"No." A smile that provided a hint of how she looked as a young woman lit her face. "I was too busy trying to make a living for Robert Junior to think about that." Her smile faded with her voice. "And then history repeated itself. He died in Vietnam while his wife was pregnant with Robby."

"I'm sorry," Wade said sincerely.

"Me, too." She cleared her throat and took a sip of coffee. "You didn't tell me how you came to have these things."

"They'd been pawned." Wade motioned toward the other two items.

She picked up the bracelet first, her expression softening once more. "This was a gift from my aunt when I graduated from college in 1950. In those days, that was considered quite an accomplishment for a woman, especially a single mother."

"And the necklace?" Wade asked.

"The cameo belonged to my mother. I stopped wearing them both after I found out how much they were worth—I worried about losing them."

"And you didn't give these things to Robby?"

"Robby?" She laughed, this time in disbelief. "What would a twelve-year-old boy do with all this?"

The smile faded and her expression clouded once more, then she looked back at Wade.

"That's not right, is it? He's all grown up now. And he's moved back into his old room in my basement. He drives me crazy with all of his late nights. And the loud music. He took these things?"

Wade nodded.

"And sold them?" Her voice was incredulous. "Well, I'll be. I think maybe that's what Megan was trying to tell me the other day."

"Before Robby died," Wade confirmed.

Helen's gaze jerked back to his. She stared at him, wide eyed, showing all the classic symptoms of shock. He felt like a rookie making his first death notification and doing a rotten job of it. There was nothing to do except take her hand. "Breathe, Helen. Just breathe."

Maybe this was why Fiona Kassell had been so protective those first couple of days. If Helen's memory was this bad, how could she be living on her own? Clearly, she shouldn't be.

Her gaze fell away and she pulled her hand from his. When she looked up at him again, the confusion was gone.

"Yes, before," Helen said quietly. "His funeral was yesterday."

"Yes," Wade agreed.

"And you're the detective."

"Yes."

"I don't know why, but I was thinking you were Megan's boyfriend, and I was glad about that. She doesn't have anyone, you know."

Though Wade knew she didn't have any close relatives, he'd wondered if she was involved with anyone. A myriad of thoughts dropped through his head like grains of possibility sifting through a sieve. How things might have been different if he'd met her a month or two ago. How he would have found a reason to talk to her if he'd come across her at the grocery store or the bank. How he liked the idea that Helen had seen him in the role of Megan's boyfriend. How he was thinking crazy thoughts that were no good for his objectivity.

NINE

A knock at the back door startled them both. "Helen?" Mcgan called.

The older woman gave Wade an intent look before answering as if warning him not to say anything about her memory lapse, her voice far brighter than it had been a moment earlier. "Come in, sweetie."

"I saw that you'd put a bunch of the apples in your car and I wanted to make sure…" Megan stopped when she noticed Wade sitting at the table. She was clearly on the job since her bright blue shirt had the Our Daily Bread insignia on it. "What are you doing here?"

"Working." He met her gaze. "What are you doing?"

"I forgot a file and came back home to get it."

"You knew that Robby was taking things, didn't

you?" Helen said, reaching for one of Megan's hands. "That's what you were trying to tell me the other day."

Megan's gaze fell on the evidence bags in the middle of the table. "Oh, Helen."

"It's all right." Helen let go of Megan's hand and stood up. "Your friend…" Her brows drew together and she made a vague gesture toward Wade. "He helped me load the car."

"I thought we were going to do that tonight," Megan said.

Helen looked around her kitchen. "I wanted to bake a cake," she said. "And this way I'll have more room."

Megan raised an eyebrow at Wade and he shook his head as Helen collected ingredients from her cabinet.

"Did you know that Robby died?" Helen asked Megan.

"Yes." Over the top of Helen's head, Megan's gaze met his, her expression at once beseeching and defiant, as though ordering him to leave and asking him to understand. Her concerned gaze went back to her friend. "Are you okay?"

"I am."

He cleared his throat. "I've got to be going."

"Thank you for coming by," Helen said politely,

as though they'd simply been having morning coffee.

"Megan, I'll talk to you later?"

"Yes." She smiled at him as he scooped the evidence bags off the table and headed out the back door. In the driveway next to Helen's property line was Megan's Lexus RX. He peeked inside as he went past. The passenger seat was rigged up with an organizer filled with file folders, and miscellaneous papers were tucked haphazardly into one of the pockets along with tissues and the other paraphernalia of someone who spent a lot of time in her car.

Wade decided to wait for her. Since she'd said she'd come home to get a file, he figured she wouldn't be very long. He could only imagine what she was saying to Helen. One thing he was sure of—Megan was being gentle with the old woman.

He leaned against the Lexus, which was warm from the morning sun and the heat of the engine. Minutes later, he heard Helen's back door close and saw a furious Megan come flying around the corner.

Megan's heart had lurched when she saw his car in Helen's driveway, and her first thought, irrational as it was, had been that something had happened to Helen. Only, paramedics would have been called, not the detective on the case.

She didn't know whether Wade had added to the stress this morning, but her first instinct was to protect her friend. "You might have remembered that she's been through a lot and so taken it a little easy on her," she said when she was a couple of feet away from him.

Coming this close to Wade was a mistake, she decided. She was too aware of the faint scent of his aftershave and the warmth in his dark eyes.

Deliberately bringing to mind Chief Egan and all the reasons she couldn't allow herself to let down her guard with this man, she folded her arms over her chest. He held her gaze like a tender hug. He smiled then, not a little one, but a lopsided one that reached his eyes and made her heart flutter.

His smile faded. "How long has Helen been losing her memory?" he asked, his voice so full of concern it brought a lump to her throat.

"A while," she admitted. "It got a lot worse when Robby came back. And this week…" She shook her head. "It's all this stress."

"Her old memories are still strong."

Megan nodded. "That's because they're wired into a different part of the brain. The more you've thought of them over time, the stronger those old connections are."

His gaze strayed toward her car. "She probably shouldn't be driving anymore."

"You're not going to make that an official thing, are you?"

He shook his head. "I have no reason to. Not until she proves she's a hazard to herself or others." He looked back at her, his smile gone and those dark eyes once more filled with the serious expression she knew. "Both she and Lou Gessner confirmed your story, by the way."

She swallowed, unaccountably relieved even though she'd known they would. "Thanks for telling me."

"Well." He looked beyond her, then patted the hood of her car. "I've got to go."

"Wait. You told me that you wanted to talk to me yesterday. Only, we never got that far last night."

"No, we didn't, did we?" He combed his fingers through his hair his expression subtly changing until the hard cop was back and his eyes had lost all their softness.

She swallowed. This wasn't going to be good.

"The shovel found with Robby," he said. "Did you handle it?"

She started to shake her head in denial, then closed her eyes, reliving the moments after she found Robby. "Probably, but I don't know for sure."

"What's your blood type?"

"O negative."

"How would you have been holding the shovel?"

Chills crawled over her scalp as she tried to bring that morning into focus. "I don't know. I just remember trying to get him flat on the ground so I could start CPR."

"And did you?"

"Yes. Even though his eyes were fixed and dilated, he was still warm. I didn't know how long he'd been down. And if there was a chance…"

Wade touched her shoulder. "Your fingerprints are on the shovel."

She heard the words, but they simply didn't make logical sense.

"Only mine? Not the killer's?"

He didn't answer that question, simply said, "You need an attorney." His voice was rough, as though his throat was dry.

Megan flushed with embarrassment. "You might have mentioned this sooner. Like last night when I was making a fool of myself talking about how you drive me crazy and you—"

"Megan, stop." He glared at her. "Just stop. This is hard enough as it is. Yeah, I like you. And I'm a cop. At the moment, that is all I can be. And I'm telling you, as a cop, hire an attorney." Something in his expression changed a bit, going from hard and frustrated to protective. "Hire the best one you can find."

With that, he walked away from her, and she began shaking. Hire the best one she could find? She wasn't even sure where to look. The lawyers she knew about were mostly experts in water and mineral rights and so on.

A glance at her watch showed she was late for her next appointment. She opened the car door before remembering the reason she'd come home—to get the file. She let herself into the house, determined to reclaim her focus. She needed to be thinking about the sixty-five-year-old who'd recently had a hip replacement and was anxious to begin riding a horse again. Instead, her thoughts circled round and round Wade's cryptic statements, and she became afraid of what he might not have told her. When she got a call from Sarah, her boss, midafternoon, her first thought was that since Sarah had lived in Natchez her whole life, she would know where to start the search for an attorney.

Megan arrived back at the office a few minutes after five. Sarah was the only one still there. She sat at one of the computer desks where they updated their charts on the computerized system they had recently installed.

Sarah held up a finger for Megan to wait while she finished her entry. A moment later, she looked up and smiled. "I keep telling myself 'I like the computer, I like the computer.' So far, it's still winning most days."

"Maybe it will be easier after the laptops come in and we don't have to do the double entry of everything."

"We can hope." Sarah stood and stretched. "Are you doing okay?"

"It's been a rough few days," Megan admitted. "And I need your advice."

"There's something I need to tell you first, Megan. I received a complaint this morning. Trent Oswald has accused you of stealing."

Megan felt herself go cold. She shook her head in denial. Accusations like this came with the territory of being in the homes of their sometimes vulnerable patients. Still, this one rankled.

Trent Oswald was the father of Lisa, whose legs had been broken in a car accident earlier in the summer. The family lived in a ramshackle house. Megan felt sorry for the girl, whose PT would have gone a lot more quickly if her dad could have been persuaded to take her to the physical-therapy center. She'd also have benefited from spending time with people other than her parents and three younger brothers.

But her dad had decided the center was for old people, since it was attached to the nursing home.

Lisa was a timid girl who acted like she was scared of her father, and Megan knew exactly what that was like. She'd never seen any signs of violence, but then, everyone had thought her own father had been a good parent, too.

"What did he accuse me of stealing?" She had never seen anything in the house of value except for the big-screen TV that dominated the tiny, shabby living room.

"A thousand dollars in cash."

Her jaw dropped.

"I know," Sarah said. "I don't think the man has ever seen that kind of cash. But what you need to know is that in addition to complaining to me, he went to the police."

Megan plopped onto the chair behind her.

"It gets worse." She picked up a sheet of paper from the counter. "Chief Egan came in a couple of hours ago with a search warrant, and they finished searching your work station a few minutes ago."

"They?"

"My nephew, Aaron, and that new detective…"

"Wade Prescott," Megan filled in.

"I'm sure they'll be waiting for you at your house."

Her lips still numb, Megan nodded her understanding. If they had searched here, of course they'd be going to her house.

"Don't worry."

That was like telling water not to flow downhill. Megan looked at her supervisor. "I'm suspended, aren't I?"

Her eyes suddenly bright, Sarah nodded. "Yeah. I'm sorry. You know company policy."

"Well." At a sudden loss, Megan looked around the large room, tears threatening.

"Don't worry about the files. I know how meticulous your notes are—I can enter it all into the computer."

Megan nodded.

"What was the advice you needed?" Sarah asked.

Megan stared at the floor, her thoughts swirling. Sarah was her friend…and her boss. Would her choice come down to the same one that Wade had laid out this morning? He liked her, but he was a cop, first and foremost. Was Sarah her employer, her boss in the same way? And would be telling her that she needed the name of an attorney be some sort of admission of guilt? This was, she decided, something she was going to have to do on her own.

"It was nothing." She lifted her bag off the floor and slung it over her shoulder.

"I'm so sorry," Sarah said as she headed toward the door.

"I know." And Megan did know that she was. Her focus in this moment, though, was on what she'd find at her house.

When Megan arrived home five minutes later, two cruisers, Wade's car and another dark blue sedan, were parked in front of her house. The sedan blocked her driveway, so she parked across the street.

As had been the case on Friday, her neighbors were out in force, gathered in whispering clusters. Anita Miller, who lived across the street and was the information highway for the neighborhood, broke away from the group and came toward Megan as she got out of her car.

Megan would have liked to have avoided her, but she was already asking, "What's going on? I asked Jim Udell when he drove up, but he wouldn't say."

Megan didn't want to lie, but she wasn't ready to confess they had a search warrant, either. "I'll know more after I talk to them."

"After what happened last week, the last thing you need is more trouble."

Megan agreed with that. Though Sarah had told her the police would be here, she had the naive idea that they might have waited for her to come home before entering her house. Instead, they were already inside, Chief Egan standing in her doorway like a sentry while he talked to someone on his cell phone. He closed it, his hard eyes on her as she came toward him. He didn't move out of the doorway, his arms crossed over his chest, effectively keeping her out of her own house.

"I want to see the search warrant," she said, holding out her hand. "And I hope you had the decency to get a locksmith to open my house instead of jimmying the door."

"Why don't you do yourself a favor, Ms. Burke, and just tell us where the money is? Things will look a whole lot better for you if you just confess."

TEN

"The search warrant," Megan repeated, reminding herself that Chief Egan wanted a rise out of her, something to add to the "probable cause" for obtaining the warrant.

He reached inside the pocket of his bomber-style jacket and handed it to her. She opened the folded sheet and read through it. The warrant authorized their search for cash—a thousand dollars, to be exact. She resisted the urge to rub away the throbbing pain behind her eyes. She supposed they could get a warrant for whatever they wanted, but the amount, though substantial, seemed a bit small to justify all the manpower. One thing she was sure of—they wouldn't find a thousand dollars. She had a couple of twenty-dollar bills stashed, but that was it.

"You haven't asked about the crime," Chief Egan said.

"I know about Trent Oswald's accusation." When the chief raised an eyebrow, she added, "I just came from talking to my supervisor, and she told me that I'd probably find you here. "

"Uh-huh." He lifted his baseball cap and resettled it on his head. "A lady like you, you don't want this kind of trouble. Save us some time and tell us where the money is."

"Since I didn't steal it, I can't tell you where it is."

"Mr. Oswald says it's missing and that you're the only one besides family that has been in the house."

"I didn't steal anything," she repeated. "Not even ten cents. How long are you going to be?"

"A thousand dollars could be almost anywhere. We could be a while." He pointed at her car. "The search warrant includes your vehicle and your purse."

Irritated with the situation in general and him in particular, she closed her eyes and mentally counted to ten. She supposed she might be able to see this from his perspective. Her being accused of another crime provided the police with the perfect excuse to search her house.

There was nothing she could do. She couldn't stop it and had no control over how long it took. Might as well cooperate. She handed him her bag, along with the keys to her car. "Knock yourself out. Remember, there are medical files in both my desk and my car, subject to privacy laws."

Her took the items from her. "Invasion of privacy is the least of your worries," he said.

Megan backed off the stoop, trying to decide what to do next. Sitting on her front step while others pawed through her things and the neighbors stood around staring had all the appeal of watching one of those stupid reality television shows. A part of her wanted to go next door to see Helen and cry her eyes out over the injustice of all this. That definitely wasn't a good idea.

From Megan's office, Wade could hear the sound of her voice as she talked to the chief. He couldn't hear her words, but she sounded surprisingly calm.

He, on the other hand, was in a rage. He disliked everything about this. The accusation of theft had provided the chief with a reason for a fishing expedition.

"I want to know what she had for breakfast, the name of her boyfriend and how old her cat is," he had said. In a nutshell, they weren't really looking for a thousand dollars.

As for those specifics, she hadn't eaten breakfast, at least not at home. She had no boyfriend, which cheered him even though he had no business thinking that. And, she had no cat. In fact, no house plants or any other living thing, which made him unaccountably sad for her.

Closing the desk drawer, he turned his attention to an armoire on the other side of the room. He opened the doors, discovering it was a desk, an artist's studio packed with supplies. This was still tidy, but not as much as the rest of the house. Colored-pencil sketches were tacked to the inside of the doors, the vibrant colors making him think of Megan's vivid blue eyes.

A pair of apple dolls sat on a shelf, dressed as an old man and an old woman. She was sitting on a rocker knitting, fine yarn somehow strung on a pair of toothpicks. He was carrying a rake over his shoulder. A sketch for the Apple Dumpling Gang logo was tacked up, as well. When Helen had told him the apple-doll project had been Megan's idea, he had thought she was referring to organizational ability, not the artistic talent revealed here.

"What are you finding?" Chief Egan asked from the doorway.

"No thousand dollars," Wade said.

"Yet. Keep looking." The chief looked over Wade's shoulder at the armoire's interior. "Lots of cubbyholes in here to search through."

"I don't think we're going to find anything. According to her bank statements, she lives well inside her means and saves money every month. She has no reason to steal."

"That you know of. Maybe she just likes the thrill of it. Lots of people do." He left the room, calling out to Jim Udell, who was searching Megan's bedroom.

Not Megan, Wade thought, fully aware he wasn't supposed to be thinking like this. Searching through her intimate belongings like this was an invasion he didn't like. He pulled out a sheaf of paper from one of the shelves and came face-to-face with a sketch…of himself.

Awareness teased like the barest touch of a feather across his scalp, and he was unable to tear his gaze away from the image that was both private and eerily familiar. He hadn't known his own eyes were filled with such longing, or that his smile seemed meant just for her. It had been, but he hadn't intended to reveal that. He also knew she hadn't wanted anyone to see this. Unlike other sketches, this one hadn't been tacked to the inside of the armoire door. He had just put the sheet on the bottom of the stack when the chief once more appeared in the doorway.

"You're not done yet?"

"Do you want fast or do you want thorough?" Wade responded, more annoyed than he should have been.

Egan gave a bark of laughter. "That's exactly what Udell told me."

He left, and Wade finished searching through the cabinet, liking the artistic aspect of Megan and wondering why she kept it hidden. When he entered the living room a little while later, he realized that not a single picture hung on a wall. Anywhere. And he wondered why.

They left the house a short while later without finding the thousand dollars or anything else that could have linked her to Robby Russell's death. Though he was aware of Megan watching him, he didn't look at her. He didn't dare. He had no business feeling all of the things he was feeling. Not until this case was over.

"See you back at the station," Egan said, heading for his own vehicle.

Wade waved and went to his own, his peripheral vision catching sight of Megan as she went inside her house and closed the door. He wasn't sure whether she was shutting herself in or shutting all of them out, but he understood her urge.

As he was opening his car door, a woman approached, carrying a toddler on her hip.

"I'm Anita Miller," she said. "We spoke the other day."

"I remember." The woman had seemed like a busybody who was more interested in everyone else's business than her own. Exactly the kind of person he didn't want to talk to right now.

"She murdered Robby, didn't she? That's why you were searching her house."

"I can't comment on the case," he said.

"What I don't understand is why you haven't arrested her. For goodness' sake, everyone knows that she did it before and got away with it."

Wade folded his arms against his chest. "Got away with what?"

"You don't know?" Anita's face brightened, as though imagining the prospect of revealing a huge secret. "She killed her sister."

Wade stared at the woman while she nearly danced in anticipation. He let several seconds pass before saying, "Megan Burke's father was convicted of that crime."

Anita's expression fell. "Oh. Well, you know what they say. The apple doesn't fall far from the tree."

"Yeah?" He opened the door once more. "In my line of work, I need facts, not rumors and gossip."

"Well, I never!" She turned around and stomped away, which suited him just fine.

What was the story with her neighbors? Why were they so ready to think the worst of her? And who was the source of information about Megan and her past? Was it someone who liked to spread rumors—or was it someone with a darker motivation? He intended to find out.

Inside, Megan went from room to room, feeling violated. Though nothing was overtly out of place, she knew things had been touched by prying, unwelcome hands. Irrational as she knew the urge to be, she wanted to wash everything down. And if that's what it took to make her feel better, why not?

She decided to start in her office, sure that's where they would have spent the most time since that's where all of her papers were. As she came into the room, she imagined she caught a whiff of Wade's shaving cream. She opened her craft armoire. She studied the shelves a long moment before discovering the sketch she had impulsively drawn of Wade was gone.

Unreasonable panic gripped her as she stared at the shelf where she was positive she had left it. Her art had always been something she kept mostly private, but this sketch went beyond that. After they'd had dinner together, she hadn't been able to get him out of her mind, or her heart, for that matter.

She hadn't had crushes in high school—she had been too depressed then, still too caught up in her mother's suicide soon after her sister's death. But she had fallen in love in college—or so had thought at the time.

These feelings she had for Wade were a thousand times more intense, ten thousand times more scary. The sketch she had drawn of him was her way of dealing with that—acknowledging both how she felt and how futile dreaming about him was. She had to remember what he had told her—he was a cop first. And she was still a suspect.

Sure her search was futile, she began looking through each stack of papers anyway. At last, there it was—tucked neatly toward the bottom of a group of other sketches. Her relief left her shaking as she stared at his beloved face while unshed tears burned her eyes. *Beloved.* Oh, how she wanted to deny that….

"Stop being stupid," she muttered to herself, wondering who had found the drawing and why it had been moved. She couldn't decide which was worse—one of the other officers finding it or Wade. Either way, it was embarrassing, and one more violation of her privacy.

She sat at her desk, tidying the items in her organizer, regaining her focus. One of them caught her eye—the check for her mortgage payment. She stared at it, unable to remember why she hadn't taken it to the bank days ago. The calendar that doubled as her desk blotter came into focus. She'd written the check the morning Robby had died. And, if she didn't get the payment made today, it would be past due.

She headed for the front door, picking up her purse and her keys along the way. At the bank, the drive up window was still open, and she had only a short wait before it was her turn.

When she pulled up to the drive-in window, she saw Neil on the other side of the glass. "How are you today?" he asked her.

She told him she was fine, doing her best not to engage in any chitchat with him. All she wanted to do was get back home and clean. She put her check in the drawer and closed it. A minute later, he put her receipt in the drawer.

"Can I do anything else for you today?" he asked.

"No, thanks."

"Give Mrs. Russell my best," he said. "And thank her for the history lesson on those old coins of hers."

"I will." Megan put the car into gear and headed for home. She wondered when Helen had talked to Neil about the old coins.

ELEVEN

Back at the station, Wade opened his files and tried to forget the unnecessary invasion of Megan's privacy. He remembered times when he had pushed just as hard to gain access to a suspect, and so he understood the chief's motives. Since the witness reporting a crime was often the perpetrator, he understood the logic about considering Megan a suspect. But, the evidence against her was so marginal that today's fishing expedition was unwarranted.

The chief might be putting stock in Megan's fingerprints being on the murder weapon, but Wade knew any defense attorney could poke huge holes through that and explain it away.

There was a killer out there, and all Wade had to do was find him. He'd started with less, and he'd been able to connect the dots. He could do it this time, as well. With the office getting quiet and every-one going home, now was the time to concentrate.

What he had was a murder victim who'd had very little contact with old friends and acquaintances since moving into Helen Russell's basement. Robby had been stealing from his grandmother and pawning the items. The one man he'd spent any time with was Neil Dillon, who claimed they hadn't seen that much of each other. Wade opened his notebook to his page of notes about that, deciding that Neil hadn't been all that forthcoming despite accusing Megan of being after Mrs. Russell's money. It was time to talk to the man again, see if his story stayed the same.

He heard a door close and looked up to see Chief Egan locking his office.

"You're burning the midnight oil," the chief said.

"It goes with the job."

"That search today was a waste of time, to all appearances."

On that, Wade agreed, though he figured saying so would be a mistake.

"I keep thinking about Oswald. It's time to press him a little harder about having a thousand dollars in cash lying around." Chief Egan lifted his baseball hat and resettled it on his head. "The man drives around in a twenty-year-old pickup that's as rusty and beat up as they come. And he has a thousand dollars?"

"All good questions," Wade said.

"I'll send one of the officers out to talk to him again tomorrow, unless you want to do it."

Wade had suspected that Oswald was just trying to take advantage of the suspicion leveled at Megan. "I've got plenty to do. Udell or Moran can handle it just fine."

"You going to be here awhile?"

"I'm going over to Neil Dillon's. He sought me out the day of the funeral. Implied that Megan could be after Mrs. Russell's money."

"You're not buying it."

"So far there seems to be nothing to support it. It's time to start looking hard at other people around Robby, and I figure his friend who knew about the coins is a good place to start."

"You're liking Ms. Burke less and less for the murder?"

"I never liked her for it at all."

"And the fact that she's a pretty young lady isn't clouding your judgment." That last was said like a statement of fact.

Wade met the chief's penetrating gaze. "I imagine you'll be the first to let me know if it is."

Egan gave one of his sudden barks of laughter. "See you tomorrow."

Wade left the station a few minutes later. It was

dark, and the air was crisp enough that he turned up the collar on his jacket. The air smelled great, as it had for the last couple of weeks—the scent of ripe apples in the air.

Wade drove to Neil Dillon's house.

A duplex a block off Main, it had a front yard badly in need of cutting and watering, surrounded by a chain-link fence. He parked, then made his way up the crumbling concrete walkway.

Both times he'd seen Dillon, the man had been well dressed, so the shabby state of his house and yard was a little surprising. Hearing the blare of a television inside, Wade rapped on the door.

The volume suddenly diminished and Neil pulled back the curtain in the front window. Wade took a step back from the stoop, and a second later the door opened.

Neil appeared, dressed in a threadbare pair of jeans and a faded concert T-shirt.

"Detective Prescott," he said.

"How are you tonight?" Wade asked.

"Fine. Couldn't be better."

Wade pulled his notebook from his pocket and absently tapped it against his hand. "I was hoping you could fill in some holes for me."

Neil nodded. "Sure. I'd be happy to do that."

"It's cold out here. Maybe we could do this inside."

"Uh, the place is a mess," Neil said. "You know how it is. You work all week, and there's not enough time to get anything done." He folded his arms over his chest, shivering a bit as he did.

"Suit yourself." Wade was curious about what was inside the house since the man would rather stand out here in the cold than have a conversation inside. At the moment, though, he had no probable cause to get inside. All he could do was drag things out and hope that Dillon's obvious chill would gain him entrance to the house.

"So, tell me again when you and Robby first met."

"Uh, we were kids. Second or third grade." Neil scratched his head, shivered and then folded his arms once more.

"And tell me, would you say you knew him well?"

For the next half hour, Wade asked every minute question he could think of about Neil's relationship with Robby. A couple of interesting things came out. Neil had never visited his friend in Denver despite professing the two were close friends. And he was inconsistent in his description of his contact with Helen Russell. He bragged about how much help he'd been to her when she came to the bank, and how he'd helped her carry things—he couldn't say what things because that would be a violation of her privacy and company policy—that she'd taken from a safety-deposit box. Neil seemed to have forgotten that he had told Wade the day of the funeral that Helen had taken the coins from the safety-deposit box. Wade let it go for the moment.

"Anything stand out in particular for you about the day Robby died?"

Neil stared at his feet for a second. "Just that we'd made plans to go out that night, you know. He was trying to put together a deal so he'd have enough cash to move out of his grandmother's place. And he expected to celebrate."

"What kind of deal?"

"I'm not sure. I mean, he was checking out a bunch of stuff, you know? Over in Telluride, mostly. Said there wasn't enough action around here."

"And you," Wade said. "A young guy like you— are you looking for more action?"

Neil's smile was sly. "Sure. I have plans. Doesn't everybody? I don't intend to spend the rest of my life in this two-bit town."

"Were you and Robby planning to get out of this two-bit town together?" Wade asked.

"Well, no. I'm just saying…" Neil shifted from one foot to the other. "He was going his way, I was going mine. Detective, is there something specific you want to ask me? Maybe about…about Ms. Burke?"

"What makes you bring her up?"

"I just thought maybe you were here because of the thing with the thousand dollars, that's all."

A chill crawled up Wade's spine. "You mean, the claim that Oswald made?"

"Yeah. That one. I just…well, I did see Ms. Burke at the bank today."

"Anything else?" Wade asked.

"No, Detective. That's it."

Wade turned and headed toward his car, leaving Neil standing on his stoop. Unless he was losing his mind, Neil was implying that Megan had deposited a thousand dollars in her account today. And, Wade hated the sick certainty that settled into the pit of his stomach.

Megan awoke the following morning, her room flooded with bright sunshine. She'd slept through her alarm.

Then it all came crashing back. She'd been suspended and had no place to go. She lay in bed a while longer, watching the light move across the ceiling, not liking the morose turn of her thoughts. What she needed was activity. None of the usual

things from painting to riding her bicycle held a bit
of appeal. Finding Robby's killer seemed a much
better idea.

She sat up and swung her feet over the edge of
the bed, testing that idea. And she liked it. The police force was small, after all, and Wade Prescott
was just one man. If she was searching, too, that
was bound to help. Plus, at the moment, she was the
only one who seemed to believe in her innocence.

Satisfied that she was onto something, she
headed for the kitchen to make a pot of coffee. By
the time she had finished eating her breakfast, she
realized she had no idea where to even begin.

She went to her desk where she sat down and
began writing random notes on a sheet of paper.
Murder needed a motive, she knew, so she wrote
that down. Who had a motive for murdering
Robby? That was the big question. He'd arrived in
town broke, singing the blues to Helen about how
he'd lost his job. Had he given someone in Denver
a reason to follow him here and kill him? How
could she find out about his life in Denver?

Maybe it was better to start with where Robby
had spent his time since arriving back in town. She
could work backward from there.

She showered, dressed and got ready to head out
when she remembered. What she really needed was

to hire an attorney. How could she have forgotten? Easy, she decided. She simply didn't want to believe that she was in that much trouble.

The Yellow Pages didn't yield any obvious choices, so she decided she would have to call Sarah.

"I hate to even ask," Megan said after they had exchanged pleasantries, "but I need the name of an attorney."

"Let me call you tonight," Sarah said. "As your supervisor, I can't do this from work. As your friend…"

"I understand. I'll talk to you tonight."

She gathered her things and headed across her yard to check on Helen. Fiona's car was in the driveway, and for a second, Megan considered skipping the visit. Helen, though, had spotted her from her place at the kitchen table and waved. So Megan crossed to the back door, wiped her feet and went inside.

"You just keep borrowing trouble, don't you?" Fiona said.

"I don't know what trouble that is," Megan replied, a little stung by Fiona's hostility.

"Stealing from your patients."

Megan's heart sank. She knew it was too much to hope that Oswald's accusation had remained a secret.

Fiona took a sip from the mug in front of her. "I suppose you got yourself fired, too."

"No."

"Then what are you doing home on a weekday morning?"

"Leave the girl alone," Helen admonished. "Do you want a cup of coffee, Megan?"

"No, Helen, thanks." Megan retreated toward the door. "I just came to see if you needed anything and to tell you that I'd drive you over to the seniors' center tonight."

Helen's brow wrinkled.

"For the Apple Dumpling Gang project," Megan reminded her.

"Oh, yes. I'll be ready."

"Okay, then. See you later."

"You need to watch yourself around that girl," Fiona said as Megan closed the door behind her.

Megan stood there a second, feeling like an outsider, the first time she'd ever had that feeling at Helen's house.

She looked over at the gate where she'd found Robby last Friday. In some ways, it seemed like only hours ago. It also seemed impossible that it had happened at all.

Squaring her shoulders, she headed for her car, and went to the bank.

As she had hoped, Neil was working. If anyone could tell her about Robby's few weeks in Natchez, it would be him.

"Hey, Neil, how are you?"

Neil's reaction caught her off guard. "What are you doing here?" he asked, his jaw tight, his voice a harsh whisper.

She pushed forward the withdrawal slip to get twenty dollars, something she could have just as easily done at the ATM but that also provided her a reason to talk to him.

When he caught sight of the slip, he said, "Oh. I thought… Well, never mind."

"Actually, I need your help," Megan said, waiting until he looked at her again. "You and Robby were friends, so I wondered, do you know what he did during the day?"

Neil shook his head and leaned toward her. "I know what you're trying to do. Divert attention from yourself and make everyone think you didn't kill Robby. You've got to be delusional to think I'd tell you anything about him."

"And you're—"

He slapped her receipt and her cash on the counter between them.

"You stay away from me, or I'll have charges filed against you for harassment."

Stunned, Megan stared at him a moment, then stepped away from the teller window. "Okay, then. It's always good to know where I stand."

Shaking, she walked out of the bank and into the crisp day, which was the coolest one yet this fall. When she got to her vehicle, she looked at the bank receipt, the number on the balance making no sense to her.

It was a thousand dollars higher than it should have been.

TWELVE

A week after Robby Russell's death, Wade was no closer to solving the case than he'd been the day of the crime. By this point in the investigation, he'd expected to have enough cold, hard facts to zero in on a suspect. His first forty-eight golden hours were long gone.

He had facts that pointed squarely at Megan, but none of them provided sufficient motive for murder even though he was pretty sure this one had not been premeditated. If it had, the killer would have come with a weapon rather than using one conveniently at hand. That suggested an argument, but no one had seen or heard anything unusual that morning. Wade figured that meant the murderer belonged in the neighborhood. But he didn't have a single fact to back up that hunch.

It was time to interview again people who

knew Robby—like Neil—and see what shook loose.

He was still waiting to hear from the appraiser about the coins he'd found that day.

His extensive notes had not turned up the cohesive pattern he expected, but one element kept cropping up. The coins. He printed the pictures of the two he'd found the day of the murder, deciding it was time to talk to Helen about them. And it was time for a follow-up interview of everyone he and Udell had talked to that first couple of days, beginning with Megan.

As happened every time he thought about her, he also remembered the drawing she had done of him. There was no point in denying that he was glad she'd been thinking about him. At least until they had searched her house. As things stood now, he wouldn't blame her a bit for being mad at him.

After he gathered up the things he needed for the day, he headed for Red Robin Lane, noticing right away that Megan's car was in her driveway. He hadn't planned to start with her, but found himself walking to her door and ringing the bell simply because he wanted to see her.

Myriad expressions crossed her face after she opened the door—surprise, pleasure, uncertainty. And then wariness, which didn't surprise him even as he admitted he was glad to see her.

"Hi, Megan," he said, thinking she looked tired. "I'm sorry you were suspended."

She wore a pair of cropped pants and a T-shirt, both as pale as her complexion. Her slender feet were bare, vulnerable-looking somehow.

She shrugged, but he doubted she felt quite that casual about it. He wouldn't have.

"Do you have time to answer a few questions?"

"My attorney told me not to talk to you."

So she'd hired one. Good. "Who did you get?"

"Robert Zimmerman. Sarah Moran recommended him."

Wade nodded. Sarah—her family had been in the town for generations. If anyone had good contacts, it would be her. "The thing is," he said, "I'm at something of a dead end, here."

He was too aware of using the ploy with her that usually worked. Getting her to help out because he was stuck. Because helping out was the right thing and she was a person who did the right thing. Because, if she was really innocent, a killer was out there somewhere.

Indecision flashed across her face. "Am I a suspect or a witness?"

"A witness."

"That could change, though, couldn't it?"

He owed her that much honesty, and so he said, "We both know it."

She came outside, much as all the other witnesses he'd interviewed on the block had done. Unlike them, she sat down on a porch step. To keep from looming over her, he sat next to her.

Immediately, he caught a whiff of her perfume. Like the woman herself, the scent was fresh, unassuming. Alluring. The air was just cool enough that he was aware of the heat radiating from her body. He'd been wrong, he decided. He should have waited until one of the other officers could come with him.

"I'm trying to reconstruct what happened that morning," he said. He flipped open his notebook. "I'd like to know more about that morning, down to the insignificant details that you may not have told me before."

"What kind of details?"

"Anything. From the time you got up, anything that strikes you as the least bit unusual."

"Like what I heard or saw?"

"Exactly."

"Trust me, nobody has thought about that more than I have." She was quiet a moment. "I remember looking outside while I drank my orange juice—it was such a gorgeous morning. I could hear the birds singing, and I was looking forward to the drive up Granger Gulch to see a patient."

She paused, and when he looked at her, he saw that she had shut her eyes. He could see the pale sprinkle of freckles across her cheeks, the fine texture of her skin and the tendrils of hair at her neck. *Focus, Wade, focus.*

"I heard a clatter by my trash cans, and I remember hoping the raccoons hadn't gotten into the trash again. And then—"

"Wait," he said. This was new. "Had the raccoons been in the garbage?"

She shook her head.

"What time was that?"

"Before I showered, so probably a little before seven. I had to be on the road by seven-thirty to make my appointment."

He made a note to compare this information to the timeline he'd drawn up.

"What about strange cars or anything like that?"

"Not that I remember." She looked at him. "You wouldn't believe how much I've been thinking about this."

"Thinking about it is normal." Since the chief viewed her as a suspect, she, more than anyone else, had a vested interest in clearing her name.

She cleared her throat and looked away, then

said, as if glimpsing the gist of his thoughts, "It's not so easy proving your innocence."

"That's why the burden of proof is on proving guilt beyond a reasonable doubt." He stood, went down the steps, then looked back at her. "I'm working on this, Megan." He had no business saying anything like that to her, implying promises he couldn't possibly keep. He took a couple of steps down the walk, then turned back to her. "I'm glad you found an attorney even though I hope you don't need it."

Megan's throat clogged at his admission. "Thanks." She knew that came out as a hoarse whisper. She kept thinking that she ought to tell him about the too-high balance in her bank account even though common sense demanded that she keep her mouth shut and let her brand-new attorney handle it.

There was one last thing she remembered. "Wade," she called. He turned around, and she tacked on, "Detective Prescott."

He turned and walked closer again, that lopsided smile almost reaching his eyes. "Putting up barriers, Megan?" he asked softly and giving her the feeling that his use of her given name was deliberate.

"I should," Megan said. "We both know I should. I thought of one more thing. You know how car exhaust smells when a car needs to be tuned up? That morning, I remember smelling that, and I think I might have heard a car in the alley about the time I came out of my house." She frowned. "Not really the kind of thing you're looking for."

"You never know. It could be important. Like the raccoons."

"Only there were no raccoons."

"Exactly." He turned away, heading down the walk. Once more, she thought about telling him about the extra thousand dollar balance in her bank account. Every value she held dear told her it was the right thing to do even though the advice from the attorney had been very clear. Don't volunteer anything. Don't talk to the police without him being present. Don't and don't and don't. What about the do's? she wondered. Do stand up for yourself. Do believe that everything would be okay if she stayed true to herself.

She remained silent, though, watching Wade go to the Miller's house a couple of doors away. He might be gathering facts, but some people, like Anita Miller, had already convicted her.

That morbid turn of thoughts did her no good, she thought, standing and going back inside. In the kitchen she sat back down at the table where her notes were scattered across the table.

In her own tiny bit of research, she had discovered there were dozens of things to consider, which gave her a new appreciation for Wade's job. Lots of people to talk to. Lots of facts to collect and interpret. She had divided hers into motive, Robby's activities, things that made her look like a suspect and miscellaneous things. Picking up her pen, she added a notation about the clattering trash cans that morning, shuddering as she acknowledged what that sound had been. She'd heard Robby being assaulted, and it hadn't registered until now.

If only she had gone to check.

If only. She had learned long ago those two words were the most futile in the English language. She'd felt guilty then, and she felt guilty now.

Under *motive,* she had written *money* and *revenge,* then had crossed out *revenge.*

After her dad had gotten out of prison, she'd spent too much time plotting how to make him pay for her sister's death since a seven-year sentence had seemed too little punishment for taking a life. Granted, she'd called it justice at the time, but it had been revenge through and through. To this day, she was grateful for the hospital chaplain that she had met at work, a man who encouraged her to turn all her hurt and her anger over to God—that justice was His in His own time, and not hers.

Because of that old experience, she was positive whatever had happened to Robby hadn't been revenge, but instead something else.

She thought hard about the noises she had heard that morning, imagining Robby and his attacker. There'd been an argument, she decided, and whoever had been with Robby had been angry enough to pick up the shovel and use it as a weapon. Who? Why?

She had the feeling that as soon as she knew the answer to one of those questions, she'd know the answer to the other.

Tired of her morose thoughts, she went outside and crossed the driveway to Helen's back door. She tapped lightly, then let herself in.

"It's Friday, isn't it?" Helen asked from the kitchen table.

"It is." Megan pulled out a chair and sat next to her, seeing that Helen was making notes on a day calendar. "I'll pick you up at six-thirty tonight." When Helen's brow puckered and she glanced back at the calendar, Megan added, "We still have apple dolls to dress."

The pucker smoothed. "Oh, yes. I keep losing track of the days, and so I decided that I needed to write things down."

"That's a good plan," Megan said, watching Helen add tonight's meeting. It said a lot about

Helen's character that she recognized she was having problems and was willing to make adjustments. "If it weren't for the notes *I* make while working, I'd never remember what I'd been doing."

"I doubt that, but thanks for trying to make me feel better. I just kept thinking it was Saturday because that friend of Robby's came by, and we had the nicest talk." She looked at Megan. "So, young lady, if it's Friday, tell me why you're home."

"I have the day off," Megan said, which was true in a way. Helen had been with Fiona yesterday when the whole subject of the suspension had come up. If Helen didn't remember, Megan decided, there was no real reason to bring it up now. What really had her attention that a friend of Robby's had been by. "Which friend?"

"The young man who works at the bank. What's his name?"

"Neil Dillon?" Megan offered, thinking of the strange interaction she'd had with him.

"That's right." Helen paused once more, this time giving her head a shake. "He said that he was worried about my coins, and he offered to help me find an appraiser. I don't need one, of course. And then he told me I shouldn't tell anyone I have them here at the house."

"That's good advice," Megan said.

"He even said that close friends and neighbors are the ones most likely to steal from a person. Can you imagine?"

Thinking about the way many of her neighbors had treated her over the last week, Megan could imagine that too easily. Still, she said, "Your neighbors are good people, Helen. I don't think you have anything to worry about on that front."

"But what if he's right? What if it was a neighbor who killed Robby? And what if they come back, thinking they can take whatever they want, even steal from me?"

Megan patted her friend's hand. "That's not going to happen."

"I think we should check and make sure the coins are still there." Helen stood with determined purpose and headed toward the back bedroom where Megan had put the tub of coins in a closet. At the doorway, Helen turned. "Well, are you coming?"

Megan followed while the cat trotted across the living room, keeping pace with Helen. When they reached the bedroom and opened the closet, Megan peered inside with Helen.

The yellow wash tub that had held the coins was gone.

"Oh, my goodness!" Helen said, her voice rising in distress. "They're gone."

Megan dropped to her knees, looking in the corners of the closet, under winter coats whose dark colors seemed to cast a deeper gloom through the closet. The tub was well and truly gone.

She sat back on her knees and looked at Helen. "Could you have put them somewhere else?" She scooted across the floor and looked under the bed, which was clear except for a few dust bunnies.

"I don't think so," she said, leaving the room.

Megan stood, looking around one last time, checking the drawers of a chest and the nightstand. A moment later, she heard Helen's footfalls going down to the basement. She caught up with Helen at the bottom of the stairs.

She was slowly walking down one wall of open shelves, looking at empty canning jars, boxes of Christmas decorations, a couple of old suitcases and a row of paperback books. Megan didn't see anything that came close to resembling the tub. She could see Helen was trembling.

Something about what she had related of Neil's visit didn't sit right, and Megan's own stomach tightened into a gnawing ache the way it had when she was a child, waiting for the other shoe to drop in one of her dad's unpredictable outbursts.

Helen opened the door to the bedroom Robby had been using. It was a spacious room with oversize windows that looked out at ground level to the backyard. Someone had cleaned and everything had been neatly put away. Helen opened the closet door, revealing only a few hanging items. The shelves and the floor were empty except for a single pair of shoes.

Helen's eyes filled with pain when she turned back to Megan.

"Do you know how much those coins mean to me?" she asked, her voice breaking. "I sat at my daddy's knee while he told me about each coin, and where it had come from and why he saved it." She crossed the room to Megan.

"What can I do to help you?"

"You can march yourself home and bring them back."

"Helen, I don't have them." Megan's voice shook, she was so shocked at the accusation.

"Robby's friend said you took them."

"I didn't." Megan's stomach heaved, and she held out a beseeching hand. Helen ignored it and left the room, then marched up the stairs, her back straight.

"Helen, let's talk about this." Megan reached the top of the stairs, following Helen to the kitchen where the old woman was removing a card from the refrigerator.

"Chief Egan told me to call him if I thought of anything. So I'm calling him."

"Because Neil told you that I took your coins?"

Helen's chin wobbled. "Yes." Her eyes clouded and she shook her head. "No." Then she pointed a finger at Megan. "I saw you bent over Robby that morning. What were you doing to him?"

"Helping him—"

"No! You were hitting him. I saw you, and I know what you were doing." Helen grabbed the phone.

"I was giving him CPR."

Helen was shaking her head, her eyes wide with fear, and backing toward the wall as though she expected Megan to strike her.

Megan motioned toward a chair. "Why don't you sit down? It'll be okay."

"You killed Robby, I know you did," Helen cried.

Megan shook her head, shock and despair competing with her need to comfort her friend.

"Get out." Helen dialed 9-1-1. "Get out!" she screamed. "You are a murderer and a thief and I never want to see you again."

Megan's heart shattered into a million little pieces. She backed toward the door, then fled.

THIRTEEN

Helen is family. My only family.

And just as Megan's mother had done, Helen had judged her based on the accusation alone without anything to support it.

Scalding tears blinded Megan before they fell, and she stumbled up the steps to her house. Each thud of her heart echoed the accusation.

Images blurred in her mind, Helen's face fading like the wash of a photograph in water, becoming her mother's eyes, her mother's voice, keeping time with the thud of her heart.

Searing pain burned through her, scorched her heart and made her want to vomit.

She pushed open the door, staggered into her house and closed the door behind her. Her gaze darted from one wall to another, walls that were carefully blank. No perfect family that existed only within those pictures.

To be sure, she looked one more time. No portraits with forced smiles. No perfectly arranged groupings that hid a fractured family.

The bare walls were marginally reassuring, as she let her back slide down one of them until her bent knees were clasped next to her chest. She wasn't eleven, and that wasn't her mother shouting at her and it wasn't her sister in the back bedroom with her lifeless eyes fixed on the ceiling.

She could get through this. She could. Get. Through. This.

Past and present still jumbled together, the memories overlaying on another in a macabre collage that included the awful day she'd come home from school and found her mother had taken her own life.

Oh, God, what do I do?

There was no answer. Only the deep well of pain that kept bubbling up inside her. She was alone again. Alone.

And Helen believed her capable of murder.

A great, shuddering sob erupted from the bottom of Megan's heart in sharp, exquisite grief.

She let her head drop to her knees.

Seconds later…hours later…she didn't know which, she became aware of pounding on her front door and someone calling her name.

She didn't care who it was. She simply wanted it to stop.

"Megan!"

The deep voice was her father's, even though she knew, in some corner of her mind, it couldn't be. He was dead. She knew he was dead because his blood money was in her bank account.

"Megan."

Who else could be yelling at her with such vehemence? No one.

"Megan!" The door opened hard, slamming back against the wall. She curled further into herself seeking a way to hide, though her paralyzed limbs would not move.

A large male silhouette dominated the doorway. He came toward her, and she shrank back, unable to take her eyes away, unable to blink because any second, her father's face would appear and the nightmare would begin all over again.

The man knelt and she cringed away from him.

He touched her, and she flinched. And then his face came into focus.

Wade.

Not her father, Wade.

"I didn't kill her," she said.

Wade took Megan's hands. Ice cubes would have been as warm. She was pale and her eyes were so dilated they looked black. He didn't ask if she was okay because clearly she wasn't. Physically, she wasn't hurt, but she was in shock and in the middle of a post-traumatic stress episode.

"I didn't kill her." This time her voice caught and a single tear spilled slowly down her cheek.

Her. She wasn't talking about now, about Robby. Megan's head dropped to her knees once more.

What in the world had happened at Helen's house? He had been talking to one of the neighbors when he saw Megan run out of Helen's house as if it was on fire. That had scared him, especially when she didn't answer the door.

Frustration gnawed at him. He wanted to help, wanted to comfort, wanted—if he was honest with himself—to hold her until this awful thing swamping her was gone. Every instinct urged him to gather her close, but everything he'd been taught told him to keep his distance. They didn't know each other that well. He was a cop, and the first rule of survival was do not get involved. Except he already was.

With sudden decision, he sat on the floor next to her and pulled her onto his lap, holding her close enough that she'd know she wasn't alone, loosely enough that she could move away easily.

Each shudder of her shoulders sank into him with the force of a slow-motion gunshot. Some nameless emotion gave way inside her, and her body suddenly relaxed. She sank into him, her face against his neck, her breath hot, her tears hotter.

God, let me be doing the right thing here. Comfort her. Oh, please comfort her.

Little by little, her sobs subsided, and though she didn't move, the tension in her body changed as though she was once more fully aware of where she was.

"What was your sister's name?" he asked her.

"Ellen." It came out as a dry whisper. After a moment, she added, "I haven't said her name out loud in…years."

"You got help, didn't you, Megan? Talked to a shrink?"

"Eventually," she admitted, her head still resting on his shoulder. "You know what was worse?" Her voice was small, soft.

"What?" he asked as gently as he knew how.

She shuddered. "The day I came home from school and found that my mom had hanged herself."

"Oh, Megan." He clasped her more tightly, the injustice of what she had endured pouring through his head with too-vivid images. He knew that she'd been eleven at the time. She never should have been a suspect, even for a second, for the crime her father had been convicted of. Nor should she have had to find her mother like that. He'd known she was alone, but the enormity of what that meant just now hit home.

"You're not alone," he whispered to her. "Never again."

"I've always been alone," she said, another shudder claiming her. "Helen thinks she saw me kill Robby."

A loud knock at the front door made Wade jump.

"Megan Burke," came Chief Egan's sonorous voice, punctuated by the sound of the door crashing against the wall.

He and Wade spotted each other at the same moment.

"What the—" Chief Egan spat out while Megan slipped out of Wade's arms.

"What's going on?" Wade got to his feet.

"I'll tell you." The chief strode toward him, pointing at Megan who still sat on the floor.

Wade's gaze fell to her. Her face was still covered with tears. She watched the chief with such resignation that a chill crawled up his back and through his scalp. He knew what the chief was here to do.

"Megan Burke, you're under arrest for the murder of Robby Russell."

"No," Wade said.

The chief's gaze pinned him. "Meet me in my

office in a half hour." He hauled Megan to her feet, handcuffing her and pushing her toward the front door. "Lock up on your way out, Prescott."

Wade knew what was coming next. His suspension. But there were things to take care of first. What was the name of the attorney she had hired?

At the front door Megan looked over her shoulder at him. He tried to smile even though he wanted to punch someone. "It will be okay," he said.

She turned her head away as though she knew as well as he did that was a promise he had no business making. They went down the porch steps while he stood in the kitchen like some fool waiting for the boulder at the edge of the precipice to crash down on him.

The attorney.

Wade turned around, his gaze landing on the refrigerator. Magnets held a coupon for pizza, a postcard of Natchez with a banner advertising the Apple Festival and a couple of business cards. The one he wanted—Robert Zimmerman, Attorney-at-Law.

Wade pulled out his cell phone to make the call. The final instant before pressing the key to connect the call he decided that would about top it for the chief—finding that his detective had called the suspect's attorney from his department-issued phone. Closing the phone, he picked up the receiver for Megan's phone and made the call. He wasn't able to speak with the attorney, but his paralegal was helpful, assuring Wade they'd immediately take care of Megan.

That completed, he still had the idea it was a puny effort to provide her with the support she needed. A bulletin board next to the phone held a list of names and phone numbers, and he was vaguely surprised at how many of the names he recognized. Sarah Moran. Caroline York. Lou Gessner. Kyle Ford.

Once more, he picked up Megan's phone, aware he was driving another nail into his own professional coffin, but the decision to call her pastor felt right nonetheless.

"Megan has been arrested for Robby Russell's murder," Wade said as soon as they were beyond the "hello's."

There was silence on the other end of the line, which made Wade wonder if the minister felt as sucker-punched as he did.

"She's been taken to the jail?" Reverend Ford finally asked.

"Yeah." Wade raked his hand through his hair, indecision once more gripping him. He had no idea how much of her past anyone else knew, and so his revealing that she'd been in the grip of a post-traumatic stress episode when he came in could be exposing her in ways she wouldn't appreciate. "She needs a friend." Lame, he thought.

"It sounds like she has one."

What kind of friend was he when he couldn't do anything except make calls and beg others to help? "One whose hands aren't as tied as mine."

"If you haven't called Sarah Moran," Reverend Ford said, "do it. I'm on my way."

"Thanks." Wade disconnected the call, and immediately dialed Sarah's number.

She picked up on the second ring, evidently seeing Megan's name on her own caller ID because she said, "You are supposed to be out enjoying this gorgeous autumn day, Megan, not hanging around the house. I thought you'd decided to take a ride up to Grand Mesa."

"It's Wade Prescott," he said.

"Wade? What are you doing calling from Megan's house? Is she okay?"

"She's not," he said. "She's been arrested."

"Oh, no.…Wait. Why are you calling from her house?"

"To make sure she gets the help and support she needs."

"I see," Sarah said. "You know, Detective, I might decide I like you, after all." With that she hung up.

And Wade once more wondered what he could do. He knew beyond any shadow of a doubt that as soon as he went to the station, he was going to be suspended. Ensuring he turned over the stone that hid Robby's killer took on new urgency because he was as sure as anything that Megan wasn't it. That thought had him wandering through her house, remembering the day they had searched it.

The house was as tidy now as it had been that day. And, he was as struck now as he had been then at how impersonal it was except for the armoire where she kept her art supplies. She was a bit like that, he decided. Her essence hidden behind closed doors.

He found himself at the doorway of Megan's bedroom, loath to enter this most personal space the way he'd done the other day. He looked around, seeing the rumpled, unmade bed, the hair raising on the back of his neck.

Trusting his intuition, he looked around once more, taking in everything, wondering what was out of place. And then he had it.

Her unmade bed. The other day, the bed had been neatly made. And today it wasn't. But the pillows didn't show any indentation, nor did the sheets look wrinkled where she might have slept.

He stepped into the room, approaching the bed,

not knowing yet what was so wrong, only certain that something was.

The corner of a yellow plastic tub caught his eye, sticking out from under the bed. He knew what he was seeing even before he knelt down and looked.

Helen Russell's missing tub of coins.

FOURTEEN

Wade was certain of two things. This scene was staged. Megan hadn't done it.

Glancing at his watch, he saw the time wasn't yet noon.

That narrowed the window of opportunity to have done this. Planting evidence, and Wade was positive that's what he was seeing, was a dicey thing. Trace evidence was almost always left behind.

Pulling his cell phone from his pocket, he called Jim Udell and Aaron Moran to come process the crime scene.

Fifteen minutes later, they arrived. As Wade watched from the front porch, he saw the neighbors gathering once again. Given what he'd learned from them all week, he knew how this looked.

All Megan had ever done to these people was be

a good neighbor. Apparently, no good deed goes unpunished.

"In the bedroom," was all Wade said to the two officers as they carried their equipment into the house.

Udell whistled when he saw the tub, "This the motive for murder?"

"Could be," Wade replied. "I want everything checked, since we know this wasn't in here when we searched on Wednesday." He added specific instructions about dusting for fingerprints on the window—he doubted the coins had been carried in through the front door. And he asked them to go over the access to the back of the house from the alley with special care.

"You're not staying?" Moran asked.

"The chief wants to see me at his office," he said, reaching for his cell phone when it began ringing. He fully expected to see the chief's number on the display. Instead, it was Helen Russell's.

"You told me to call you if I saw anything strange or remembered anything," she said.

"That's right."

"Can you come over?"

"Sure," he said, heading through Megan's front door and down the steps. "I'll be right there."

As he crossed the lawn, he saw Helen sitting at

the table where she could see outside. The neighbors were still standing in clusters. She waved at him, motioning for him to come in.

He climbed the back steps, wiped his feet on the doormat and entered.

"What's going on, Mrs. Russell?"

"That's what I want you to tell me," she said. "All those police cars again."

"I was hoping you could tell me what happened a little while ago when Megan was here."

Helen's gaze turned inward. "Megan was here this morning?"

Wade sat across the table from her. This was more strange by the moment. He vividly remembered that Megan had said that Helen had accused her of killing Robby. If Helen had been the slightest bit upset, she didn't show any signs of it right now.

"She was," he replied. "Do you remember that *I* was here this morning?"

"You were?" Helen shook her head. "Chief Egan came to see me. But maybe I called him. I can't remember." She sighed, then looked at him. "The truth is, I think I'm forgetting a lot of things."

"You've had a pretty stressful week. Forgetting happens." Reassuring her was the only thing he could do at the moment, though forgetting like this was a long way from being okay. He cleared his throat. "Why did the chief come see you?"

Helen shook her head. "I'm not sure."

"You said that you might have seen something? Or remembered something?" he prompted.

"Oh, yes." She shifted slightly and pointed out the window. "That strange car has been here all morning."

Wade's gaze followed the direction of her pointing finger to where a nondescript gray sedan was parked.

"I think it's Neil Dillon's car," Helen said. "He just sits there and watches." She pointed to the desk calendar on the table in front of her. "I saw it the other day, too, because it says so right here. I wrote it down. His car was here last Friday, and it's been here every day since then." She looked at him. "I think that's strange when he just sits there, don't you?"

"I do."

She frowned. "Something else happened this morning." Her voice faded and she shook her head. "Something…"

Frustration and compassion warred inside Wade as he watched her. He wanted to know what had happened this morning when Megan was here, but he could equally see that Helen didn't remember and was upset by the fact that her memory was fuzzy. He could only imagine what that might be like.

He looked once more out the window. He saw Neil get out of his car and go over to one of the clusters of neighbors, who immediately included him in their circle.

"He and Robby were arrested for shoplifting when they were in junior high," Helen said. "I remember being so mad. I made Robby pay back every penny."

"What did they steal?" Wade asked, his attention still on Neil.

"CDs, I think. It was a long time ago."

Wade's cell phone rang, this display showing the call was from Chief Egan. He flipped open the phone. "Prescott."

"I'm waiting, Detective. And my patience is getting shorter by the minute."

"I'm on my way." *But not before I check on Udell's and Moran's progress next door and then talk to the neighbors,* he thought. He disconnected the call and said to Helen, "I've got to go. Is there anything I can get for you? Anyone I can call?"

She shook her head.

"Maybe your friend Mrs. Kassell?"

"No." Helen looked once more at the calendar. "I

want to rest today. Megan is taking me to the seniors' center tonight, and we're going to finish dressing the apple dolls. You know about that, don't you?"

"Yeah. The Apple Dumpling Gang."

"It was Megan's idea, you know. Dress them up as grandmas and grandpas."

"I remember." This was at least the second time she'd told him that story, he thought as he headed for the back door. "I'll see you soon."

Outside, the neighbors were still talking, and as Wade watched, Neil Dillon slipped away, heading for his car. As soon as he was in it, he drove away. Wade noted the time on his watch—a little after noon—wondering why the man wasn't at work at the bank.

He went into Megan's house and found Udell and Moran still in the bedroom. Moran had dusted for fingerprints and was methodically lifting and labeling them.

"Anything interesting?" Wade asked.

"We found shoe prints outside several of the back windows," Udell said. "They've been photographed. The impressions aren't deep enough to do a cast, but I think we have some decent photographs."

"Could they be Megan's—Miss Burke's?"

He shook his head. "Not unless she has feet as

big as yours." He met Wade's gaze. "This whole thing was staged, if you want my opinion."

"I think so, too."

"The chief called looking for you," Moran said. "I'm surprised you're still here."

"I'm heading over there right now," Wade said.

He crossed the street to where his car was parked— it was in front of the yard where the neighbors were still talking. He couldn't wait to hear what they had to say to him this time. And sure enough Anita Miller broke away from the group and came toward him.

"We saw Chief Egan take Megan away," she said. "Did he arrest her for murdering Robby?"

"You'll have to talk to him about the charges," Wade said.

"And you're searching her house again." She shook her head. "I never imagined I'd be one of those neighbors who says, 'She was such a nice person, and I never suspected she was capable of this.' But here I am."

"Capable of what, exactly?" Wade asked.

"Murder," she said. "And all of it over that sweet Mrs. Russell's coin collection that Megan stole. And as if that's not enough, to think she stole from Trent Oswald and then had the audacity to deposit the money in her own bank account. There ought to be a law."

"There are laws," Wade said. "What coins are you talking about?"

Anita put a hand over her mouth, her eyes widening in surprise. "I shouldn't have repeated that."

"Repeated. So someone else told you. Who?"

She looked around at the neighbors, then dropped her voice. "I really shouldn't say."

"You really should," Wade said quietly. "Or I'll have you charged with obstruction, and aiding and abetting and—"

"Well, Neil Dillon, that's who," she said indignantly, backing away from him. "There's no need to get so testy. I'm just a concerned citizen trying to do the right thing."

"Yeah, I can see that," Wade said, opening his car door.

At last the dots were beginning to connect plus one he hadn't heard before—the supposed deposit of Trent Oswald's money in Megan's account. Wade didn't believe in coincidences. There had to be a reason Neil Dillon had known about that and the coins. Before Wade went to the station, he intended to find out what that reason was.

Megan sat in the holding cell, determined not to fidget, though she could barely sit still, as she repeated to herself, "Everything will be fine." She didn't know how, but if she gave up on that idea, she'd be screaming.

The expression in Wade's eyes gave her a slender thread to hang on to. He'd been as shocked by her arrest as she had been. More, because she'd known that Helen was going to call Chief Egan. Wade, though, had been caught flat-footed.

And he'd held her when she needed it most. That had to mean something. She didn't know what, but something.

This was not the moment to be thinking about the fact that she was in love for the first time in her life. The sheer terror of feeling this way was reason enough to not want it. What if her feelings weren't returned? What if she ended up all alone after this was over, anyway? What if it all turned out badly and she went to prison? What if she got out of this okay and he turned out to be a closet abuser like her father had been? What if—

"Hi, Megan."

She jerked her head up, so lost in her thoughts that she hadn't heard the door open. Reverend Ford stood on the other side of the bars, the door with its small window that led to the booking area closing behind him. He pulled a straight-backed chair close to the bars, as though he was accustomed to talking to people here. Maybe he was.

"Hi," she said. "What are you doing here?"

"I came to see you."

"Why? How did you know I was here?"

"Why—because I figured you could use a friend, knew you'd need a little prayer. How—a friend of yours called me."

She stared at him. Only two people knew she was here if she didn't count her gossiping neighbors. Helen and Wade.

"Helen called you?" Once that would have been the most logical assumption. After today, she was no longer so sure.

Reverend Ford shook his head. "My neighbor."

"Wade—Detective Prescott?"

When he nodded, a balloon of warmth expanded through her chest, and for the first time since she'd been brought in here, she relaxed a tiny bit. Things would be okay.

"Did you get your phone call?" he asked.

"Yes." Now that she thought about it, her conversation with Bob Zimmerman's paralegal had been strange, as though the man had already known what had happened. Could Wade have been responsible for that, as well?

"Is there anything else I can do for you?"

"I'm worried about Helen," Megan admitted. There was no point in telling Reverend Ford about her accusation, especially since she wasn't at all sure Helen would even remember what happened this morning. "This morning was pretty upsetting for her—"

"I'll go see her. Maybe convince Fiona to go with me."

"Yes. She'll need a ride tonight, anyway, to the seniors' center."

"You'll be home in time to take her," he said.

"Fiona should take her." Megan's chin quivered as she remembered that even if she did get out, Helen probably wouldn't want to see her. "I wish I had your confidence."

"Faith," he corrected. "Are you ready to pray now?"

"Yes," she said. "I think I am."

He scooted his chair closer to the bars, reaching for her hands.

Megan closed her eyes and let the sound of his deep voice wash through her. The words mattered less than the feeling of calm they generated. If God was everywhere, He was also in this place right here and right now. She wasn't alone.

The metal door behind Reverend Ford opened just as he was saying, "Amen." Sarah Moran came through, followed by Chief Egan.

Once more, Megan was surprised, especially

when Sarah came right up to the bars and reached for her. "Are you okay? What can I do for you?"

"One of you needs to leave," Chief Egan said. "In fact, letting either one of you back here—"

"Oh, for Pete's sake," Sarah said. "What do you think we're going to do in here? Plan a breakout? We're here to support a friend while she's waiting for her attorney." She folded her arms over her chest and faced the chief. "We're both staying."

"Sarah—"

She smiled. "Yes, Carl?"

He raised his hands, shook his head and backed toward the door. "Okay."

"Sensible choice." The door closed behind him. "What in the world happened?" Sarah asked. "When Wade called me and said you'd been arrested—"

"Wade called you, too?" Megan asked, incredulous.

"Whoops. You should ignore that. Carl probably won't be too happy about that."

Megan's legs turned watery, and she plopped onto the end of the cot, her gaze going from Sara to Reverend Ford. Wade had called them both, and they both had come. And she'd been so sure she was as alone as a woman could be.

Once more, that balloon of warmth filled her chest. And this time, it wasn't quite so terrifying.

FIFTEEN

Wade had imagined arriving at the station with Neil Dillon handcuffed and confessing to Robby's murder and framing Megan. Though Wade was positive that was what had happened, he hadn't caught a break. Dillon wasn't at work—he'd called in sick. And he wasn't at home.

All that meant he wasn't going to have the exoneration he'd wanted for Megan when he talked to Chief Egan.

"Hey, Wade," Caroline said from her desk when he came through the door. "Chief is waiting to see you." In a whisper, she added, "He's on a tear."

The chief must have seen him come through the door because he yelled, "Get in here."

Wade headed for his office.

"Close the door behind you," Egan said when Wade crossed over the threshold. "First, would you like to explain why Udell and Moran are at Megan Burke's house?"

"I found Helen Russell's missing coins under Megan's bed. I figured you'd rather they process the scene than me."

Egan's eyes narrowed. "Any chance we could have missed those coins the other day?"

"None, sir."

"Uh-huh." He drummed his fingers against his desk. "You've got about thirty seconds to tell me why I shouldn't suspend you."

Wade swallowed and met his boss's gaze. "In all honesty, I can't do that. I've fallen in love with the woman you've arrested, so my objectivity is shot."

He hadn't intended to say that, nor had Egan expected him to admit to it, since his eyes widened before his features settled into an even deeper frown. Wade's heart pounded harder than it had the first time he'd chased down a suspect. He was in love. A lifetime of memories flashed in front of his eyes as he stood there, beginning with the daily stress he'd seen in his parents' marriage, most of it because his dad had been a cop, and ending with his own vow that he'd never subject a woman to what his mother had endured. The idea of being in love with Megan and not having a life with her was incomprehensible.

"You have anything else to add, Detective? Or are you simply going to stand there like you've been struck by lightning?"

In a way, he had been, Wade decided, reclaiming his train of thought. "As it stands, though, the case against her is so flimsy I'd be surprised if the D.A. would indict her."

"It's your grave, but maybe you'd like to elaborate."

"One, Mrs. Russell is having major memory lapses."

"Alzheimer's?"

"I don't know, but her short-term memory isn't reliable. She may have accused Megan of killing Robby—"

"She says she watched it."

"Maybe that's what she thought she saw when Megan was administering CPR. And maybe the next time you talk to her, she won't remember anything."

"She seemed fine to me."

"Talk to her again," Wade said, then held up a second finger. "As of this morning, the neighbors know all about the missing tub of coins. Now, since Mrs. Russell just figured out they were missing this morning, and since that fact hadn't been reported to me until this morning, that suggests someone is feeding them information for the rumor mill."

"Continue."

Wade held up another finger. "Third, those coins just happen to show up in Megan's house today, on the very day they're reported missing. I'm telling you, they were a plant, left in such a way that you'd think you were following a treasure map with X marking the spot. Megan Burke is a smart woman. If she'd taken those coins, she sure wouldn't have put them halfway under her bed."

"Do you think Udell and Moran will concur?"

Wade knew that Udell thought so, but he also figured it was better for the chief to hear it from someone else. "You'll have to ask them."

"Mrs. Russell or the Burke woman could have told the neighbors."

"Not likely," Wade said. "Plus, why would they? Finally, there's the Trent Oswald accusation about the theft. According to one of the neighbors, Megan deposited a thousand dollars in her account the day we searched her house."

"Some criminals are stupid. Maybe she's one of them."

"Yeah, some are. But so far, we don't have any motive for her to steal because she's not broke and she doesn't appear to be a person who steals for the fun of it," Wade said. "Today, I learned the person at the bottom of the rumor mill is Neil Dillon."

"He works at the bank, doesn't he?"

"That's right. But, the way this was related to me was as though we already knew about it. I haven't verified that it's true yet."

"Another frame?" Egan waved for him to sit.

"A theory," Wade said, sitting across the desk from the chief.

"Dillon was the one who helped carry the coin collection out of the bank the day Mrs. Russell took it out of the safety-deposit box. At a conservative estimate, the collection is worth at least twenty thousand dollars. Unlike some things, coins would be fairly untraceable and easy to sell off. Mrs. Russell told me today that Robby and Dillon had been caught shoplifting when they were kids. What if they never quite grew out of that penchant for the easy buck? What if Robby and Dillon planned to take the coins, sell them off and split the proceeds?"

"That would explain coins at the scene of the crime."

Wade nodded. "I think they got into some sort of argument and Dillon picked up a handy weapon— the shovel. Things got out of hand, Dillon whacked him over the head and took off with the coins. Then, along comes Megan with the skeleton of her sister's death hanging over her, and he figures he's got a patsy if we can be made to think she's got a motive."

"All right, Prescott, why didn't you bring him in?"

"I couldn't find him," Wade said. "He's not at work and he's not at home."

"Get Udell and Moran to help you and go find him," Egan said. "I don't need her attorney breathing down my neck for not charging her yet."

Wade didn't need to be told twice.

After what had seemed like hours, Bob Zimmerman arrived, looking as he had when she'd met him the other day—harried but in control. He wasn't surprised to see Sarah. After exchanging pleasantries, she excused herself, promising she'd be back.

"I'm going to start with a simple question," he said. "And we'll go from there."

"Okay."

"Did you kill Robby Russell?"

"No." The day she'd hired him, his paralegal had warned her these questions could come just this bluntly. They still shocked her.

"Physically harm him in any way?"

"No."

"Okay. Tell me what happened."

Megan did as best she could, admitting that she'd been extremely upset after Helen's accusation and her misinterpretation of what she'd seen that fateful morning.

"Have you told this to anyone else?"

"No. I may have said something about Helen to Wade Prescott, but—"

"What about the money? Did you tell the police about the money in your account?"

"No. You told me not to."

"Good."

"The only thing that makes sense to me is that someone is framing me," Megan said. "But I can't imagine why."

"That's easy," he said. "A sleight of hand to make your mark look the other way while you steal something bigger—metaphorically speaking." He paused in front of the closed metal door. "Don't get too comfortable. I expect you're going home within the hour."

True to his word, that's what happened, without bail being posted because no charges had been filed. Megan didn't believe it when he walked her into the afternoon sunshine. She'd been so sure that she'd be in jail for days.

"One thing, Megan. Detective Prescott found a tub of old coins in your house."

"No."

"A couple of officers went in to take fingerprints and process the scene. They're finished, but you may have a mess in your house."

"Helen's coins were found in my house, and they didn't file charges—not even for stealing? That makes no sense."

Bob opened the passenger door for her. "I've known Carl Egan a long time. If he thought you stole those coins, you would have been charged."

While Bob drove her home, he told her to keep a low profile, assuring her that they had a good handle on things but weren't out of the woods yet, that they might not be until the police arrested someone else for the crime.

"Do you want me to come in with you?" he asked.

Megan looked out the window to her house that was basked in afternoon sunlight. "No. I'll be fine."

She wasn't sure how she'd sleep there tonight, but at the moment, she had to prove to herself that she could walk into her own home without being afraid.

As she opened the car door, Bob said, "Egan plays things close to the vest, but he gives me the feeling he knows he made a mistake in arresting you."

"It would have been nice if he'd figured that out sooner," she replied, thinking of the humiliation and raw fear that had suffocated her this morning. It would be a long time before she'd be able to forget the looks in her neighbors' eyes. At one level, she didn't care what they thought of her. At another, she cared because she didn't want to forever be known as that woman who was arrested once for murder. In her case, twice.

After he let her out and drove away, she realized that she had left this morning without a key or any identification. She might need a key, but whoever had brought the coins in hadn't needed one.

She shivered, regretting that she'd told Bob she'd be okay. Since Helen had a spare key, Megan's choices were down to standing there in the middle of her own walk or facing Helen. She would rather have a hole open up and swallow her.

Feeling as unsure of herself as she ever had an as adult, she trudged up Helen's driveway to the back door. Helen wasn't at her seat in front of the window, so Megan wasn't even sure she was at home.

Still, she knocked on the back door, then stepped away from it. A moment later, she heard Helen talking to someone inside the house and the sound of her footsteps as she approached the door.

"Well, my goodness, Megan," Helen said with a smile when she opened the door. "Since when are you standing on formality and knocking on the door?"

Megan crossed the threshold, and Helen hugged her. "Did you get off work early today?"

Helen doesn't remember. Megan didn't know whether to laugh or cry. How could she be angry even for a moment about this morning when her friend didn't remember? "No. I didn't go to work today. But I need my spare key. I'm locked out of my house."

"Of course. Come in."

"Who were you talking to, Helen? Am I interrupting?"

"You remember Robby's friend, Neil." Helen closed the door behind Megan.

Megan looked beyond Helen and saw him sitting at the dining-room table. He stood and came toward the kitchen.

"It's a surprise to see you, Megan," he said. "I'd heard you'd been arrested this morning."

Good news travels fast, Megan thought, and bad even faster.

Helen looked from Megan to him and then back again. "Megan, arrested? Well, that's clearly not right or she wouldn't be here now." Helen shook her head. "Honestly. All the rumors on the block lately. Theft and murder. It's enough to make a person think they lived in a big city."

Megan swallowed the lump in her throat at

Helen's statement since she didn't seem at all aware that she was talking about things that had happened to her.

"Tell me, Megan," Neil said, folding his arms over his chest. "Which do you like better? Living in a big city where nobody knows you? Or living in a little town where everybody knows your business."

"I've liked living here," she said, finding his attitude odd and his questions even odder. "You're not so invisible here."

"Really?" The corner of his mouth lifted slightly, not a smile, but a snarl. "You think you have to live in a big city to go unnoticed?"

"I…I don't know."

He pointed at her, then did smile, a mean accusing smile. "But you should. Remember the other night in the diner? You were standing right next to me, and you didn't even see me."

The night she and Wade had eaten together. "You're right," she admitted, hoping to appease him. "What can I say?"

"You're sorry?" He said it as though she owed him one.

She nodded. "Okay, then. I'm sorry." She looked back at Helen. "I really do need to get my key."

"Of, course, sweetie." She went to the pantry

and opened it, pulling Megan's key off a hook on the inside of the door.

"She didn't think you were so sweet this morning, did she?" he said. "Not when she thought you'd killed her grandson."

So this was what was beneath his insipid surface. Mean jabs.

Her temper at the surface, Megan turned on him. "Stop it. Who do you think you are, saying things that upset Helen?"

He shrugged. "It's not like she's going to remember later. She's been forgetting a lot of things lately."

"That doesn't give you the right to upset her now."

"I was Robby's friend!" he said, almost shouting.

"I know you are," Helen said soothingly. "We're all upset that he's gone."

"Where has he gone, Helen?" he sneered.

"Why, you know as well as I do. Denver."

Neil looked back at Megan and smirked. "See? She's not going to remember a thing."

"I'll remember," Megan said. "And I think you should go."

"I'm not going anywhere." He put his hand behind his back, and when he brought it back, it held a gun. "Not until you confess to killing Robby."

SIXTEEN

Megan looked from the gun to Neil to Helen, who looked as shocked as she felt.

"Are you crazy?" Megan asked. Her palms turned sweaty in an instant, but despite the fear, she was mostly mad.

He shook his head, his eyes glittering, making him look more animated than he'd ever been. "No. They don't sell handguns to crazy people." He waved it. "I'm definitely not crazy."

Maybe, but that he was so cavalier about this made her worry. Getting him calm was the first priority. Or maybe the second since the first was figuring out what to do and how to get Helen out of harm's way.

"And what happens after I confess?" Megan asked.

He smiled that mean, jabbing smile once more.

"It will be the thing that drove poor Helen over the edge. She's going to shoot you."

"I would never," Helen said, taking a step toward him. "Bean you over the head with a rolling pin, maybe—"

He grabbed Helen by the arm and pushed her toward one of the kitchen chairs. "Enough of that. Both of you. Sit down."

Megan took Helen's hand, which was as cold and clammy as her own, and clasped it reassuringly. She squeezed back.

Megan looked closely at her friend, saw that her eyes were sharp. She'd like to believe that Helen was with it right now.

Helen sat at the table, picked up a pen, and began writing on her desk calendar.

Megan leaned against the table, hiding Helen's activity from Neil. "I think there's a hole in your plan."

"It's a good plan, and everyone will believe me. She believes you killed Robby, you know."

"Humph," Helen said from behind Megan.

"How can you explain her shooting me with your gun?" Megan made a point of looking at his hands. "Your fingerprints all over it."

"They'll wipe off."

"Like they did on the shovel the morning Robby died."

Neil's eyes glittered once more. "Sounds good, but you can't prove that."

"No, I don't suppose I can."

"You sit down, right there," he commanded. "You need to write down that you killed Robby."

Since he sounded more upset, she sat. The only thing that had been on the table was the desk calendar, and it was no longer there.

"What do you want me to write on?"

"Paper, of course." He glared at the table as if just now realizing that there was none.

"I'll go get you some," Helen said.

"Do you think I'm stupid?" he asked. "I'm not going to let you out of my sight. There's paper here somewhere."

His gaze darted around the room, beads of sweat popping out on his upper lip. "This was a good plan," he repeated, glaring at Megan as if daring her to contradict him.

She shrugged and looked away. "If you say so."

Outside, she saw a shadow moving up the driveway, and when she looked out the window, saw Wade coming up the side of the house. Rescue was at hand, but he didn't know that Neil was in here and armed and getting more agitated by the second. There had to be a way to warn Wade.

She looked at Neil, then at Helen, letting herself

be upset with the situation, praying her voice would carry outside.

"No, you're right, and I was wrong," Megan said a little hysterically, waving a hand. "It was a good plan." She clapped a hand over her eyes and sobbed. "I don't know what I was thinking."

"It's about time somebody noticed," he said.

"Noticed what, dear?" Helen looked up with that expectant expression she often had, and for the life of her, Megan couldn't tell if her friend was leading Neil on or oblivious to the danger.

"That I'm smart. At the bank, they treat me like I'm a nobody." He waved the gun. "But I showed them. That extra thousand dollars in your account—they'll never figure out how I did that."

"You did that?" Megan asked, angry all over again and forgetting that she'd planned to be hysterical enough that Wade would hear loud voices and hopefully figure out that something was wrong.

Neil didn't notice, though, instead he looked proud of himself. "Yeah, I did that. And I planted the tub of coins under your bed because they're the only thing that link me to Robby…" His eyes narrowed.

"You killed my grandson?" Helen surged out of her chair, the desk calendar held in both her hands.

Her sudden move surprised Neil because he stumbled back, off balance.

It wasn't enough advantage, but it was something. Megan sprang out of her chair, lowered her shoulder and plowed into him. "Get out of the house!" she yelled at Helen. "Go get help!"

Neil didn't fall, but staggered back like a drunk.

"I'm not leaving you." Helen began hitting him with the desk calendar while Megan hit his arm, trying to make him drop the gun.

The kitchen door burst inward.

"Drop it."

Wade came toward them, his weapon held steadily in both hands, his eyes as fierce as his command had been.

"Set your gun on the floor," he repeated to Dillon.

The fight went out of Neil, and he let the gun fall to the floor. No sooner than he had, Wade kicked it away, putting Neil's arms behind his back and handcuffing him.

"He killed Robby," Helen said, her voice surprisingly calm. She was still staring at Neil.

"I heard that part." Wade's voice was gruff as though he was trying hard to hold in his emotions. His gaze collided with Megan's. "You okay?"

She nodded, still trembling from her confrontation with Neil. He knew exactly how that felt since it had scared a decade off his life when he'd realized that Neil was in here with Helen and Megan and that he had a gun.

With effort, he tore his gaze from Megan's to look at Helen, who was still glaring at Neil.

"I always thought you were a bad influence on my grandson," Helen said. She took a step backward then, the fight going out of her and her chin quivering. Her shoulders began to shake. "He killed my Robby."

Megan put her arms around Helen, her tenderness with the older woman tightening Wade's throat.

"I didn't mean to," Neil whined. "It was an accident."

"Shut up," Wade said, taking his cell phone out of his pocket and dialing Chief Egan's number. The minute he came on the line, Wade said, "I'm bringing Neil Dillon in."

"He confess?"

"Yeah," Wade said. "He did." He disconnected the call and hauled Neil to his feet. "You two going to be okay?" he asked looking from Megan to Helen and back again.

"Fine," Megan said, taking her friend's hand. "I think we need a cup of tea. And we've got some catching up to do."

He pushed Neil toward the door, then turned to

look at Megan one more time. "Would it be…" He had to clear his throat. "…okay if I came by later?"

Her eyes very bright, she nodded.

"Okay, then."

"I want a lawyer," Neil said in his whiney voice.

"And you'll get one," Wade said, urging the man toward his car. When he came back, Megan wouldn't be a suspect or a witness any longer. Just the woman he was in love with. The woman he wanted to spend his life with.

Impossible that it had happened so fast, especially since he'd planned that it would never happen at all.

Maybe God had listened to his prayers after all.

Booking Dillon went smoothly enough, but the process took hours. By the time Wade got back to Megan's house, the sun had been down a long time, and it was well past dinnertime. Megan's house was dark, which didn't surprise him. He figured that she was probably next door with Helen. The shade was down over the window where Helen kept watch over the neighborhood, but he could see that a light was on.

He knocked lightly on Helen's door and heard footfalls inside.

A second later, Megan smiled sleepily when she saw him. She was in stocking feet and her hair was mussed. No woman had ever looked more beautiful to him. In that moment, he knew he wanted to see her with this particular expression every day for the rest of his life.

"I'm sorry I'm so late," he said.

"That's okay. We just got back ourselves. Tonight was the grand finale of dressing the apple dolls."

"Ah." She held the door open for him, and he came into Helen's tidy kitchen, which showed no sign of the struggle that had taken place earlier. "How did that go?"

"Okay." She wrapped her arms around herself. "I wasn't sure if I'd be okay about all the gossip, but…" Her voice trailed away, and she shrugged. "You can't control what other people think—or say."

He agreed, but he was still angry about that on her behalf. "Helen's gone to bed?"

Megan nodded. "She's tired."

"But you didn't go home?"

After a moment, she shook her head, her gaze not quite meeting his. "I'm still getting over the idea that Neil broke in." She managed a grin. "I think I need a big, mean dog."

"That would do it." What he had in mind for her was a lot more personal than a big dog.

"Is Neil in jail?"

"He is," Wade confirmed. "I imagine his attorney

will try to make bail, but that won't happen until the arraignment."

"So I could go home."

"Yep."

"I went there to change my clothes. There's fingerprint dust all over the place."

"I'll help you clean it up. I know a trick or two."

"Do you?" Something in her voice changed, teasing him. Her gaze searched his face, then her voice sobered. "You look tired."

"I could say the same about you."

"It's been a long day," she said.

"A good day." No one had been hurt, and the bad guy was in jail. He counted that for a lot. "Maybe you want to stay with Helen tonight."

Megan looked around the kitchen. "I already decided I would. This was a tough day for her, too. She shouldn't be alone."

She hadn't talked about this morning, and maybe she wouldn't. But he knew that Helen had accused her of terrible things. And yet, here Megan was, already beyond that.

"How do you do it?" he asked.

"What?" Her confusion was understandable since he'd given her no clue of where his thoughts were headed.

"Let go of everything that happened earlier today. You had to have been hurt by what she did to you this morning."

"She doesn't remember," Megan said.

"But you do."

Her brilliant eyes met his. "Only if I choose to dwell on it, and I don't."

"So how do you do it?" he asked.

"By remembering the first Bible verse I ever memorized. 'So you can see that his faith was working together with his deeds; his faith became perfect by what he did.'" She swallowed. "What kind of friend would I be if I held against her something she didn't mean?"

"In case nobody has told you lately," he said to her, reaching for her hand, "you're pretty amazing."

"Thanks." She touched one of the buttons on his jacket. "You've been okay, too."

It was time to tell her good-night and leave, though he didn't want to.

"Good night, Megan."

Her brilliant eyes shimmered and she tipped her head. "'Night." She pushed open the door and stepped onto the stoop.

As he walked down the steps, he sensed her behind him, and he turned to look. Something in her expression gave him the idea that he'd somehow hurt her feelings. "Megan?"

When she met his gaze, her vivid eyes at once hopeful and wary, he knew he couldn't leave her like this. In a single step, he was back on the stoop and eye level with her. He leaned over and kissed her.

She sighed, and thankfully, kissed him back.

He hadn't intended their first kisses to be like this, over so fast when he wanted to linger. He kissed her again, this time taking his time at it, and enjoying the moment. Overwhelmed suddenly by the idea this moment had been nearly lost, he pulled her closer, burying his face in her soft hair. When she sighed and her arms came around his back, the worry that had tied him in knots these last days loosened and fell away. This was just about perfect.

"I'm starving," he said a moment later, lifting his head so he could look at her. "They serve breakfast all night long at the diner. Come eat with me."

"Is this just food?" she asked.

Since there'd been that whole date-not-a-date thing going the last time they ate together, he laughed. "Nope. This is a date."

"I'm not dressed for a date," she said.

He shook his head and smiled. "Okay, then, it's just food." He took her hand. "Will you go out with me tomorrow night?"

"On a date," she clarified.

"On a date," he said, "where I pay and polish my shoes and everything."

She pretended to think. "Okay. Real date tomorrow night, just food tonight. Let me go get my jacket."

"You might want some shoes, too." He could hear her laughter as she disappeared inside the house.

He led her toward the car, this moment feeling right to say what was in his heart. He'd been here all these months without meeting her, and he didn't want to loose another moment.

"I should warn you." When she looked at him, he added, "After our date tomorrow, there's a good chance I'm going to tell you that I love you."

"Really?" She turned those vivid eyes on him, happiness illuminating them. He'd done that for her, and he felt about ten feet tall. "After, hmm?"

He started the car. "I just thought I should warn you, so I don't scare you off or something."

"Just so you know," she said, "I never tell a man I love him on the first date."

He looked over at her, sensed she was teasing him and liking it.

"What about the second?" he asked.

"It could happen," she murmured.

"Then maybe tonight should be our first date," he said.

"I was thinking more along the lines that the other night had been our first date."

He turned toward her, his heart beating hard enough to pull a freight train. "Put me out of my misery, Megan."

"I love you," she whispered.

"Thank God." He held her face in his hands, thankful beyond words. "I love you, too. I think I have since that very first day."

* * * * *

Dear Reader,

One of my favorite things about romance novels is the idea that, in the end, everything is going to work out as it should. I usually come away feeling inspired by the adversity that a hero and heroine have overcome. That, it turn, reminds me of this lovely quote from Robert Louis Stevenson (remember reading *Treasure Island*?): "Keep your fears to yourself, but share your inspiration with others."

I think many of us are looking for the same thing—to be inspired and to have this idea that, in the end, everything is going to work out. For me, that comes through looking at possibilities rather than worries, through my best rather than just enough to get by, through doing what's right rather than what's easy.

My hope for you is that you find inspiration and find your happy ending. May God's blessing be always with you and yours.

Sharon Mignerey

QUESTIONS FOR DISCUSSION

1. Megan and Wade both have secrets in their pasts that affect their current relationships. What differences do you see in those?

2. Family violence eventually led Megan toward faith. What Biblical examples reinforce this idea?

3. A case of family violence and the injustice of it took Wade away from faith and made him question the idea of a personal, loving God. What Biblical references might have helped him through that dark time in his life?

4. Do you see anything in the relationship between Megan and Helen that reminds you of the relationship between Naomi and Ruth?

5. One of the ideas raised in this book is the loss of reputation through gossip. Does this fit with your experience, and if it does, what are some ways to reduce gossip in your own life?

6. Based on Megan's situation, do you think it's possible to prove innocence? If not, why not?

7. What Biblical references about judgment are applicable to this story?

8. One of the issues in this story is Helen's memory loss and how it affects her friendships with Megan and others. How do experiences in your life parallel or differ from the experiences Megan has in dealing with Helen?

9. What are some examples of Wade's conflict between being a good detective and his need to believe in Megan's innocence?

10. Megan refers to the life-insurance money she inherited from her father as blood money. Why do you think she didn't give it away or otherwise spend it, rather than simply keeping it?

11. What examples demonstrate Wade resolving his crisis of faith?

12. Megan believes that God's will can only be for good. How does that fit with your ideas? What Biblical references support her view and yours?

REQUEST YOUR FREE BOOKS!
2 FREE RIVETING INSPIRATIONAL NOVELS
PLUS 2 FREE MYSTERY GIFTS

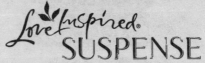

Love Inspired.
SUSPENSE

YES! Please send me 2 FREE Love Inspired® Suspense novels and my 2 FREE mystery gifts (gifts are worth about $10). After receiving them, If I don't wish to receive any more books, I can return the shipping statement marked "cancel". If I don't cancel, I will receive 4 brand-new novels every month and be billed just $4.24 per book in the U.S. or $4.74 per book in Canada, plus 25¢ shipping and handling per book and applicable taxes, if any*. That's a savings of over 20% off the cover price! I understand that accepting the 2 free books and gifts places me under no obligation to buy anything. I can always return a shipment and cancel at any time. Even if I never buy another book, the two free books and gifts are mine to keep forever.

123 IDN ERXX   323 IDN ERXM

Name	(PLEASE PRINT)	
Address		Apt. #
City	State/Prov.	Zip/Postal Code

Signature (if under 18, a parent or guardian must sign)

Order online at www.LoveInspiredSuspense.com
Or mail to Steeple Hill Reader Service:
IN U.S.A.: P.O. Box 1867, Buffalo, NY 14240-1867
IN CANADA: P.O. Box 609, Fort Erie, Ontario L2A 5X3

Not valid to current subscribers of Love Inspired Suspense books.

Want to try two free books from another series?
Call 1-800-873-8635 or visit www.morefreebooks.com

* Terms and prices subject to change without notice. N.Y. residents add applicable sales tax. Canadian residents will be charged applicable provincial taxes and GST. Offer not valid in Quebec. This offer is limited to one order per household. All orders subject to approval. Credit or debit balances in a customer's account(s) may be offset by any other outstanding balance owed by or to the customer. Please allow 4 to 6 weeks for delivery. Offer available while quantities last.

Your Privacy: Steeple Hill Books is committed to protecting your privacy. Our Privacy Policy is available online at www.SteepleHill.com or upon request from the Reader Service. From time to time we make our lists of customers available to reputable third parties who may have a product or service of interest to you. If you would prefer we not share your name and address, please check here.

LISUS08

Love Inspired SUSPENSE

TITLES AVAILABLE NEXT MONTH

Don't miss these four stories in December

DOUBLE THREAT CHRISTMAS by Terri Reed
The McClains

She had means, motive, opportunity—of course
Megan McClain is accused of double homicide. But Megan
isn't willing to spend Christmas in jail for a crime she didn't
commit. And nothing Detective Paul Wallace says will stop
her from finding the killer herself—at any cost.

SEASON OF GLORY by Ron and Janet Benrey
Cozy Mystery

Why would anyone poison a holiday tea party?
Andrew Ballantine knows his would-be killer is still
in Glory, North Carolina. And to thwart the culprit,
he'll have to get well. Which means letting lovely nurse
Sharon Pickard closer than he'd like....

SUSPICION by Ginny Aiken
Carolina Justice

When Stephanie Scott is mugged, longtime admirer Sheriff
Hal Benson rushes to the pharmacist's aid. But then drugs
go missing, and Steph's reputation is at stake. Will Hal risk
his future to save hers?

DEADLY HOMECOMING by Barbara Phinney
All of Northwind Island believes Peta Donald murdered
her ex-boyfriend. No one thinks she's innocent except
newcomer Lawson Mills. And since no one's looking for
the real killer, only *they* can find the truth—before
the killer acts again.

LISCNM1108